The blood was beating so hard in my ears, it was a few seconds before I could hear anything. Then I heard the sound of scuffling near the front door and footsteps approaching the back room.

I slipped the money under the bottom step and felt around for a weapon. I picked up a large Coke bottle and, carrying it like a club, I started up the steps again. I didn't want to be trapped in the basement.

When I got to the top, I could hear someone at the far end of the back room near Mr. Kerr's desk rummaging around, bumping into things, and knocking account books and pencils onto the floor.

The scuffling sound died near the front door, and a voice called, "Mouse, where are you?"

The figure standing over Mr. Kerr's desk said, "Looking for the bag of money."

It was Mouse's voice.

By Jon Hassler

STAGGERFORD
SIMON'S NIGHT
THE LOVE HUNTER
A GREEN JOURNEY
GRAND OPENING
DEAR JAMES
ROOKERY BLUES
NORTH OF HOPE
THE DEAN'S LIST
THE STAGGERFORD FLOOD
THE STAGGERFORD MURDERS
THE NEW WOMAN

Young Adult Novels
FOUR MILES TO PINECONE
JEMMY

FOUR MILES TO PINECONE

by

Jon Hassler

BALLANTINE BOOKS • NEW YORK

RLI: <u>VL 5& up</u>
      IL 6 & up

A Fawcett Book
Published by The Random House Publishing Group
Copyright © 1977 by Jon Hassler

Published in the United States by Fawcett Books, an imprint of The Random House Publishing Group, a division of Random House, Inc., New York, and simultaneously in Canada by Random House of Canada Limited, Toronto. Originally published, in hardcover, by Frederick Warne & Co., Inc. in 1977.

FAWCETT is a registered trademark and the Fawcett colophon is a trademark of Random House, Inc.

ISBN 978-0-449-70323-6

Printed in the United States of America

www.ballantinebooks.com

First Ballantine Books Edition: March 1989

OPM 29 28 27 26 25 24 23 22 21 20

for Mike, Liz and Dave

FOUR
MILES TO
PINECONE

Chapter 1

Summer is over.

I hope I never have to live through another one like it.

First, I flunked English. Then there was the break-in at the grocery store that put Mr. Kerr in the hospital and me out of work. And finally, a three-hundred-pound goon tried to run me over with a truck.

I'm not the scholarly type, so you may be wondering why I'm sitting here in the public library with a ballpoint pen and a notebook.

It all started back in June, on the last day of school. Mouse Brown and I stood by our lockers comparing report cards. I had an F in sophomore English and so did Mouse. I knew my parents would have a fit, and I asked Mouse to go with me to see Mr. Singleton. I thought we might talk him into changing our grades.

But Mouse said no. He said flunking English didn't make any difference to him. He said he was thinking about quitting school now that he had turned sixteen. He said he'd had a fantastic job offer, and if he liked the work his school days would be over for good. I tried to picture Mouse working, but I couldn't do it. He's like his dad. I've never known him to shovel snow or mow a lawn or set out the garbage. His mother does it all.

So I went alone to see Mr. Singleton. I found him sitting in his classroom, cleaning his glasses with his tie, and squinting at thirty empty desks. Without his glasses he looked ten years older, and very tired. The sound of city traffic drifted up through the open windows. The room was hot.

"Thomas," he said, "I know why you're here. You are less than satisfied with your grade."

"I'm in a state of shock," I said.

"All is not lost, Thomas. Pull up a desk and be seated. We shall talk. Nothing is hopeless."

"That's what I came to hear," I said. I sat down.

"Hope is a thing with feathers that perches in the soul." Mr. Singleton is forever quoting dead poets. He put on his glasses and gave me the same repulsive smile he always gives students who talk out of turn or carve on desks. It's the only smile he's got, and he shows a lot of crooked gray teeth. He's the only teacher I know who can discipline a student simply by smiling at him. You'd rather behave yourself than look at those teeth a second time.

2

"Mr. Singleton," I said, "I deserve better than an F in English. I did great on all your tests. I know everything you teach, and here you flunk me. How can you get away with that?"

I was coming on strong. His smile faded.

"Please do not question my judgment," he said. "Now it's true that you know a great deal about what I teach, but you have one great weakness—one vast flaw—in an otherwise adequate mentality."

"What's that?"

"You lack perseverence, my good young man."

"What's that?"

"Perseverence is another word for handing in assignments. Would you care to estimate the number of written assignments you failed to hand in during the year?"

"I know I skipped a few. Ten or twelve."

"Guess again."

"Maybe more. Maybe twenty. But I had a job, Mr. Singleton. I couldn't always find time to do the assignments."

"Guess again."

"Twenty-five?"

He opened his grade book and said, "Look at this," and pushed it across his desk. "Forty-seven," he said.

"Forty-seven?" I said. I pretended to be surprised, but I knew he was right. I had decided early in the year that I wouldn't trouble myself with English assignments, because English always came pretty easy for me, and I figured I could get by with at least a C by simply showing up for class and taking the tests. English assignments, if you take them seriously, can really cut into your free time.

He insisted I look at his grade book. With a dirty fingernail, he was pointing to my name. Sure enough, except for the A's and B's I got on tests, every little square after my name was blank. Forty-seven of them.

"Those A's and B's don't average out to F," I said. I wasn't about to give up.

"Those forty-seven empty squares stand for forty-seven F's. A very low average, indeed. Perhaps the lowest average in the history of Donnelly High School. Perhaps the lowest in the city of St. Paul. For all I know, it may be the lowest of any sophomore in the western hemisphere."

He was getting nasty now, so I decided to quit reasoning and play on his sympathy—even tell a lie or two if I had to. I told him my father would come after me with a leather strap. I told him I might lose my job at the grocery store. My mother might die of grief. I told him I might have to drop out of high school because I couldn't afford the extra time it would take to make up his course.

When I got to the part about my mother, he realized I was spreading it pretty thick. That's when he gave me a big horrible smile.

"Thomas," he said, "I have a plan. That F can be changed to the B you're capable of earning—if you will write one long story in a mature style and free of mechanical errors. I will give you the whole summer to finish it. If you bring it to me on the first day of school next fall I will change your grade."

4

"But in the summer I work full time in the grocery store. I'm not sure I'd have the time to work on English."

"If you wish to pass the course you will find the time. It will be up to you. It is your one chance."

"Well, maybe I can work it out. Just tell a story in writing—is that it?"

"Yes. A story of some length."

"What length?"

"Forty-seven pages," he said. And smiled.

Chapter 2

When I left Mr. Singleton, I was already twenty minutes late for work. I ran out the front door and across Marshall Avenue—dodging six lanes of traffic. Then I turned and ran as far as the police station where I cut through the alley for three blocks and entered Kerr's Grocery through the back door.

Kerr's Grocery is a one-man store—two aisles of groceries and a meat counter across the back. Most of his life Mr. Kerr handled the business all by himself. But now he was getting old, and he wanted somebody like me around so he could rest his feet. He lived alone in the two-room apartment above the store, and sometimes he went upstairs for a nap while I was on duty.

In the back room I put on my green apron, then I

walked out to the front. Mr. Kerr was standing behind the check-out counter with one arm draped over the cash register and his other hand under his apron, scratching his stomach. It's a big stomach for such a short man.

"Explain yourself," he said. He was grumpy.

"I had to stay after school and talk to a teacher. This was the last day of school, and I had something to clear up."

"Is it cleared up?"

"Not really. I'll have to—"

"Clear it up in September. Between now and then, see if you can get that case of corn flakes open."

Breathing loud through his nose, he shuffled to his desk in the back room, while I cut open the case of corn flakes. The sultry air hung in the little store at ninety degrees, and none of it stirred. It was one of those days when the slightest effort makes sweat roll down to your eyebrows and drip off the end of your nose.

The moment I finished putting the corn flakes on the shelf, Mr. Kerr called, "Now clean the display in the front window. It's full of dead flies."

So I removed the cans of soup, which had been standing in the window since midwinter, and I replaced them with a fruit-juice display.

When I finished that, Mr. Kerr called, "Now polish the glass on the meat case. It's full of greasy finger marks." Mr. Kerr had the uncanny ability, even with a wall between us, of knowing the exact moment when I ran out of things to do.

I polished the meat case, and when I finished that, he called, "Pick over the grapes. A lot of them are turning bad in this heat."

"How about us having a Coke first?" I asked.

"Pick over the grapes."

Mr. Kerr was gruff. His fat lower lip always stuck out and he never smiled. But after working for him for a year now, I knew his gruffness was only an act. Behind his sour appearance, he was basically a kind man, and everyone in the neighborhood seemed to like him. If a customer was short of cash or had an orange turn rotten on the way home, Mr. Kerr always gave him a loan or a fresh orange.

He paid me twenty dollars a week when I worked part time, and sixty dollars a week in the summer. He let me drive his old car to make deliveries every Tuesday and Saturday. "If we're going to be the widow's friend," he used to say, "then we've got to deliver. And God knows, most of the widows in the world live in this neighborhood."

When I had freshened up the grapes, I got two Cokes out of the pop cooler and took them to the back room and handed one to Mr. Kerr, who was working on his account books.

"Thank you," he said, and he took a long swig. "You're very generous with my merchandise."

Then the supper-hour business started up. I sold sardines and crackers to Al Sorenson, a head of lettuce to Mrs. Mahoney, and five dollars' worth of frozen dinners to Mrs. Brown. There were others, some I knew, some I didn't. I was working the cash register like a typewriter when Mr. Kerr came up front to take over.

"Six o'clock," he said. "You better just take twenty minutes for supper. Lots of folks will be in tonight to shop for the weekend."

"Okay," I said. "I'll run both ways."

"Take my car. Too hot to run."

I took his keys, ran out the back door, and hopped into his car. It's an old Ford with a stick shift. My driver's license was only about three months old, and driving gave me a great feeling. I pulled out of the alley and drove to the stoplight on Marshall. While waiting for the light to change, I shifted into neutral and listened to the engine idle. I gunned it a couple of times and turned on the radio.

When the light finally turned green, I shifted into third gear by mistake and jerked out to the middle of the intersection where the engine died. The drivers' training car at school had an automatic shift, and I'm not too handy with the stick yet. There was a driver behind me and another in front of me trying to turn left. They both lay on their horns. I got so flustered I didn't get the car into the right gear until the light changed again, and by that time horns were honking at me from all four directions. But once I got going, I screeched away, leaving a thick trail of rubber on the street.

I drove past the high school, turned down our street, and parked in front of our apartment building. There aren't many houses in this part of St. Paul— mostly apartment buildings and small stores—and the building we live in is pretty much like all the rest: old and stained with soot and pushed right up to the street, with no front yard.

I locked the car and was inside the front door before I remembered the rotten report card I was carrying in my pocket.

Chapter 3

My parents take a greater interest in my grades than I do. I had known them to get upset over D's, so there was no telling what this F would do to them.

I stood in the hall outside our apartment on the third floor and planned how I was going to break the news. My dad works nights in a factory. I would wait until after supper when he left for work, then I would hand the report card to Mother on my way out. I would tell her I was in a hurry, and it wouldn't be a lie. Mr. Kerr was expecting me back.

But the first thing Dad said when I opened the door was, "Let me see your F." He was sitting in the living room in his undershirt, watching the news on TV. When I hesitated, he snapped his fingers. He's a man of few words.

"How did you know about my F?"

"Mouse's mother called." I don't think my mother has ever met Mouse's mother in person, but they call each other all the time to compare sons.

It was a grim supper. Instead of food, Mother had my report card on her plate. She studied it the whole time and kept asking me the same question: "Thomas, why?"

I explained how I understood English, and Mr. Singleton knew I understood English, but he was hung up on assignments, which didn't have much to do with understanding English. I said the assignments were busywork. Useless. Dumb.

Dad, who eats in his undershirt, told me to watch my talk, and speak of Mr. Singleton with more respect. He said, "Do you think I could make a living at the factory if I understood my work but never actually did it? Just stood around all day understanding it? By the time a fellow's your age, he ought to know that there's more to life than just sitting around understanding things. You've got to get to work and prove what you know. That's what life is—making use of what you understand. If you don't know that by this time, your brain must be damaged. Is your brain damaged, Thomas?"

"Don't be sarcastic," my mother said. "Thomas needs punishment maybe, or advice, but not sarcasm."

"Don't butt in," said Dad. "When I'm upset I'm sarcastic. And it looks to me like it's too late for advice. Does that F in English mean you can't be a junior next year?"

"No, nothing like that." I told him I could probably have the grade changed to an A or a B simply by doing some written work before school started in the fall. I made it sound like a simple matter.

"What kind of written work?" said Dad.

"Just a story. Mr. Singleton said I should write a story." My stomach turned over when I thought of forty-seven pages.

"How much work will it be?"

"Oh, not much," I lied. "I'll just make up a story and write it down."

"How long does it have to be?"

I hated to say.

"How long?" Dad insisted.

"Forty-seven pages."

"Forty-seven pages!" Dad began to laugh. "Why, that's a better punishment than I could have thought of myself. I'd like to meet that Mr. Singleton. I like that man's style." He pushed his chair back and had a good laugh. Mother, too, began to chuckle. Knowing the F could be changed was a great relief to them. They seemed to be going out of their minds.

I told them Mr. Kerr wanted me back by six twenty. I got up to leave.

"Be home by ten thirty, Thomas," said my mother.

"Put half your pay in the refrigerator when you get home," said Dad.

I drove back to the store thinking about money. I had hoped Dad would let me keep more of my salary now that I was sixteen, but he still expected half for himself. That would be about four hundred dollars by

13

JON HASSLER

the end of the summer. And if he kept collecting after
school started again, that would be another four
hundred by next spring. To say nothing of the eight
hundred I had given him over the past year. What did
he need all that money for? He had worked at the
factory ever since I could remember, and he must
have been making at least enough money to support
three people. But every Friday night I was expected
to put half my pay in the covered dish in the refrigerator—that's our hiding place—and every Saturday
morning whatever I put in would be gone. I couldn't
figure out what he spent it on because his only pastime
seemed to be sitting around in his undershirt watching
ball games on TV.

Mouse Brown always said he'd be burned up if his
old man got half his pay, but I wasn't. Even if I was,
it wouldn't do much good because once Dad made up
his mind he seldom changed it. Anyhow, why should
Mouse be burned up? Half of Mouse's pay would be
half of nothing. Mouse never worked.

Speak of the devil. At the stoplight on Marshall
Avenue Mouse Brown was sitting on the curb reading
a paperback and smoking a cigarette.

"Hey, Mouse," I called from the car.

"Hey, Tom. What you doing after work?"

"Nothing. How about you?"

"Nothing. I'll stop by the store. About ten?"

"Yeah, I'm through about ten. We'll go to Tilbury's
for a hamburger."

"Right," said Mouse. He went back to reading.

Chapter 4

By nine o'clock the steady stream of shoppers had tapered off, and Mr. Kerr had gone to his desk in the back room. The only shopper left was an old lady reading the labels on practically all the cans in the store. I sat on the check-out counter watching her. She was working her way through the jam, picking up various jars, reading the small print, and putting them back on the shelf. In the wrong places. Her shopping bag hung limp on her arm, so I knew she hadn't tried to steal anything yet, but she looked suspicious to me. I went back and told Mr. Kerr she looked like a thief.

"What do you mean, a thief!" he said. "I saw her when she came in. She's no shoplifter. I know a shoplifter when I see one. Now go back out there and dust the canned goods."

With a wet rag I started wiping off the canned fruit. By this time the old lady had moved on to the sardine and tuna shelf. Every time she picked up a can she looked at me out of the corner of her eye. Ten minutes more of this and I went back to Mr. Kerr again.

"If she's not a shoplifter then she's crazy," I said. "Whichever she is, I think she ought to leave."

"You're a busybody, Tom. You're an old lady yourself. Now get back to work and leave the poor creature alone. She's lonely. She hasn't much to do. If she's happy in my store, she's welcome."

When the old lady got to the produce display, it was too much. She went through the lettuce, head by head, squeezing and jabbing, and pulling off the outer leaves. Mr. Kerr was touchy about his lettuce, so I went to the back room and told him what she was doing.

"My lettuce!" he said. "Follow me. I'll show you how to handle savages."

He approached the old lady and said, "Lady, might I suggest you take off your shoes and stockings and get in there with your bare feet?"

I had heard him say that to lettuce rippers before, but I had to chuckle anyhow, it's such a great line. The old lady tipped her head back and looked down her nose at Mr. Kerr. She switched her shopping bag to her other arm, patted it a few times, and then hurried out the door.

I reminded Mr. Kerr that she was a lonely old lady with nothing else to do.

"And I'm a lonely old man with a rack of lettuce," he

muttered as he picked up the scattered leaves from the floor. "I've got pity for her kind until they get into my lettuce. There's something about lettuce that attracts old ladies. When they get their hands on it, you have to be tough with them much as you hate to." He puffed and whistled through his nose, cleaning up the floor. "Now that old biddy will probably go home and brood all weekend about what I said. I'm not proud of what I said, but, by Godfrey, a man has to protect his lettuce."

With his hands full of lettuce leaves, he shuffled off to the back room, snorting and mumbling.

About ten o'clock Mouse Brown came into the store while Mr. Kerr and I were counting the money from the cash register. He sat on the check-out counter and watched us.

After we had stuffed the money in a sack, Mr. Kerr asked Mouse if he knew how to count.

"What do you mean?" said Mouse. "Of course I know how to count."

"Well, you were watching us like you never saw anybody count before. Didn't your father ever tell you it was impolite to watch people count their money?"

"No, he never told me that. Listen, my dad talks a lot about money, but he's never said anything like that. All he ever says about money is he wishes he had some. He wishes his unemployment check was bigger. Listen, he's unemployed, you know." When Mouse talks, he has the curious habit of telling his listener to listen. "At least most of the time he's unemployed. He works for the street department once in a while, and

JON HASSLER

you know what a two-bit outfit that is. He works when
there's an emergency—like cleaning up after parades.
When there's a parade with horses in it, he's sure of
work. Otherwise he just paints street markers once in
a while, or helps put up stop signs. No, he never talks
about politeness."

Mouse is quite a talker. He sat on the counter telling
Mr. Kerr about arguments his family had over
money—who spent it and what for—and about the
poor meals they had at home ever since he could
remember, either sardines or frozen dinners.

"If things aren't so good at home," Mr. Kerr said,
"what are you doing to help the situation? Do you have
a job for the summer?"

"No, sir. No job. Work kind of goes against me.
Listen, I'm still a schoolboy, Mr. Kerr, and summer is
a time for a schoolboy to rest up from the year gone by
and store up energy for the year to come. Look at Tom
here. He works hard all the time and what happens to
him in school? He gets a red F. Listen, when I see a
schoolboy get a red F, I say there's a boy that
overextends himself. Doesn't know his own limitations. Listen, I know my limitations, Mr. Kerr. I have
no summer job."

"Don't try to kid an old man," said Mr. Kerr. "You
work harder thinking up excuses to be lazy than Tom
does stocking shelves."

"Listen, I figure there's a lifetime of work ahead of
me when I graduate from high school, so I'll just hang
around over the summer, enjoying myself while I
can."

Mr. Kerr didn't think much of Mouse. "Look here," he said, "what I'm doing for Tom. Maybe it will motivate you."

He counted out twenty dollars and handed them to me and said, "Starting tomorrow it's full-time work and sixty dollars come next Friday."

"Fine, Mr. Kerr. Thanks a lot," I said.

"Promise me you won't spend it on parasites."

"Don't worry," I said.

Chapter 5

Mouse and I went to Tilbury's Cafe and ordered hamburgers. While we waited, I said, "Thanks a lot for telling your mother about my F. My folks ambushed me when I got home."

"Listen, what did you expect me to do? Pretend I was the only one who flunked?"

"You could have just said there were others. You didn't have to tell her who."

"She asked me who. Listen, you're turning into a worrier, you know that? What's so serious about one lousy F?"

I told him what it would take to get my grade changed—a forty-seven-page story. I asked him how many assignments he had turned in.

"None that I can recall."

"Then you'll have to do the same thing—write forty-seven pages."

"Are you kidding? Listen, maybe you don't remember what I told you this afternoon. I'm quitting school. I've got a job lined up."

"But you told Mr. Kerr you were going back to school."

"I was giving Mr. Kerr a line. I got a job. Night shift, you might say. Easy work and good money."

"Where do you work?"

"It's more or less a secret. My boss doesn't like me to say too much about it, because everybody and his brother would come around wanting a job. It's that kind of a job. A lot of guys would snap it up in a minute if they had the chance. You would yourself. It pays a lot better than sixty a week, I can tell you that. Of course, I haven't started yet, but I'm going to work tomorrow."

"How much will you make?"

"It will vary from week to week. Listen, let's change the subject. Does Mr. Kerr take in a sackful of money like that every day?"

"No, Fridays and Saturdays are good days, but the rest of the week is pretty slow."

"But still, he must have quite a bundle stashed away, don't you think?"

"I never thought about it."

"Listen, it stands to reason. An old bachelor like that. He's got nobody to spend it on. Where does he keep that bag of money?"

"He banks his money."

21

"But I mean like tonight. The bank isn't open."

"I don't know. I suppose he keeps it in his desk in the back room."

Our hamburgers came, two apiece, each with a paper-thin slice of pickle. It took Mouse less than a minute to finish eating. He devours food like a hungry dog, and he never seems to grow. He's been small and skinny all his life, that's why he's called Mouse. That, and the unhealthy gray color of his skin, which he gets from reading science fiction paperbacks all the time, or sitting around pool halls smoking.

He watched me closely as I started on my second hamburger. I tore it in two and gave him half before he asked. I hate a beggar.

He gulped it down and said, "Tom, you ought to give some thought to quitting school. Doesn't it bother you to think of two more years of that nonsense?"

I shrugged. He was right. Two years seemed like eternity.

"Listen, guys our age ought to be out making something of themselves, instead of sitting around Donnelly High School trying to see molecules through a microscope. Listen, do you know what my biology teacher had us doing one day? He had us looking at a drop of spit under a microscope to see if anything was swimming in it. That was the day I decided I had enough of school."

"Did you see anything?"

"Listen, nothing swims in my spit. But Shirley Buckingham saw something swimming in hers, and she was sitting right next to me. It gives you a creepy feeling to be sitting next to somebody whose spit has things swimming in it. I never felt the same about Shirley Buckingham after that. And to think I almost asked her for a date one time."

"I haven't thought about Shirley Buckingham since we were in the fourth grade," I said.

"Why, what happened in the fourth grade?"

"That was the year she told me she was my girl friend. And I believed her. I went around thinking of her as my girl. And then I learned from four or five other guys that she told them the same thing."

"So you got jealous."

"No, that was about the time my dad gave me a new bike. A new used bike. It had a basket. In the fourth grade a girl doesn't compare to a bike with a basket."

"Listen, Shirley Buckingham still doesn't."

When we got up to leave, Mouse asked me if I would pay for his hamburgers.

"What? You mean you ordered hamburgers with no money to pay for them?"

"Don't get all upset. I'll pay you back double when my money starts rolling in."

On the way out of Tilbury's, Mouse pressed the coin release on the cigarette machine, but it released no coins.

Walking home, I said, "Mouse, I need an idea for a story. I can't quit school, so I have to write forty-seven pages. But I haven't the foggiest idea what they'll be about."

"All right," said Mouse, "let's see. How about this? Write about a man who has a guardian angel with a body."

It was about what I expected from all that sci fi he reads.

"Not your regular kind of angel, like the sisters in grade school used to tell us about," he said, "but this angel has a body of a man and the wings of a bird. And the man he watches over would have to carry him around on his shoulder all the time, and if the man is tempted to do bad things, the angel would peck him on the head and flap his wings. The angel would have the beak of a bird, you see."

"Too wild."

"Or listen, how about a story concerning an old lady who works in the emergency room of a hospital, and every night when she goes home from work she takes along tiny bottles of blood she gets from accident victims. She likes to remember these accident cases, see. And instead of knickknacks around the house, her shelves are lined with little bottles of blood. Keepsakes."

"You're crazy."

"No, seriously, Tom, if you have to write a story, write something original. These are some of my best ideas. I think them up all the time."

"You read too much."

"Or how about this? You have a man who is normal most of the time, see, but every seven days he turns into another kind of creature for twenty-four hours. One time he's a rat, the next time he's a spider, and so forth. You could write a lot about that. How much do you need? Forty-seven pages? Listen, I can see it now. This fellow has been dating this girl, see, only he's very careful so she won't see him on his bad day—she doesn't know about his problem. Then one day they meet accidentally in an elevator or someplace, and she watches him turn into a ground hog."

"I couldn't write that kind of stuff. My mind doesn't work that way."

"So I'll write it for you."

"What?"

"Listen. I'll write you a forty-seven-page story. A masterpiece. I work nights, right? In the daytime I'm free, right? So I type a page a day for forty-seven days and give it to you and you put your name on it and pay me forty-seven dollars."

"Forty-seven dollars!"

"Well, isn't it worth that not to go through Singleton's English class again? If you work for Mr. Kerr you won't have time to write."

I thought it over. "Mouse," I said, "if you do the whole job—think up the story and type it—and if Mr. Singleton accepts it I'll pay you twenty dollars."

"Chicken feed."

"Twenty-five."

"Chicken feed."

"That's as high as I'll go. That's over fifty cents a page."

"Twenty-five is an insult. Do you think Tolkien wrote stories for twenty-five bucks? His talent was priceless, so mine is worth at least a dollar a page."

"Who's Tolkien?"

"Man, you're really out of it, aren't you? He wrote about the hobbits. Hey! There's Bob Peabody."

A car approached us, and Mouse shouted, "Hey, Bob!" The car stopped and Mouse got in and waved to me as the car sped away.

The apartment was hot. I put ten dollars in the refrigerator and watched TV for a while. Then I went to bed and thought about the car that had picked up Mouse. I had caught a glimpse of the driver, the man Mouse called Bob Peabody, and he looked familiar.

I fell asleep and dreamed that an old lady in a police uniform with a shopping bag over her arm was stopping traffic on Marshall Avenue and asking each driver for his license. The licenses were report cards. One of the drivers was Mouse, and when she saw his report card she made him get out and walk. Mr. Kerr came along, followed by Mr. Singleton. She permitted both of them to continue driving, although she studied Mr. Singleton's card for a long time and he gave her his worst smile. The man named Bob Peabody was next. She made him walk. Then it was my turn. I was driving Mr. Kerr's Ford. She took such a long time reading my card that I woke up before she decided. It was still dark.

I suddenly remembered who Bob Peabody was. He had been a senior in high school when I was in junior high, and he made a name for himself robbing stores and getting caught all the time. He spent most of his senior year in jail. The police let him out every morning to go to class and they locked him up in the afternoon. After he graduated, he went to work for an auto-parts warehouse. He drove a pickup for them, making deliveries to places that called in for parts, and every time he made a delivery he would swing by his house and drop off a part for a car. By the time they caught on to what he was doing and checked his garage, he had a new car just about built. He had it all welded together, complete, except for the engine.

Tonight was the first time I had seen Bob Peabody since he got out of the reformatory.

Chapter 6

My alarm went off at seven. I dressed and went to the kitchen, where I poured a glass of milk and put bread in the toaster. I looked in the covered dish in the refrigerator—as I expected, my ten dollars was gone. I balanced two slices of toast on my glass of milk, and with two caramel rolls in my other hand I went out into the hall and up two flights of stairs to the roof.

Mother and Dad were sitting in their lawn chairs on the flat, tar-covered roof, as they do every morning when Dad gets home from work and the weather is good. Dad was reading the morning paper, and Mother was writing a letter in her lap. I sat on the tar and spread my breakfast out on a page of newspaper. I asked Mother who she was writing to.

"To Chad and Gert," she said. "We heard from them

yesterday. They were wondering if you were coming up to visit them this summer."

Uncle Chad is a brother of my dad's. He never left the north woods. He and Aunt Gert own a small resort on Leaf Lake near Pinecone, a little town not far from the Canadian border. Until I started working for Mr. Kerr, I had always spent a week up there every summer, helping out a little around the resort and doing a lot of fishing and swimming and hiking in the woods.

"I bet it's nice up at Uncle Chad's place now," I said, feeling the heat of the sun rising from the tar around me. "This time of the morning up at Uncle Chad's it's still chilly. The grass is still wet with dew, and the fog is hanging over the lake." I could see Leaf Lake in my mind's eye as though I had been there yesterday.

"Where did you go after work last night?" asked Dad from behind his newspaper.

"To Tilbury's for a hamburger, why?"

"Who was with you?"

"Mouse. I was home by ten thirty."

Dad said nothing.

"Well, by ten forty-five at the latest," I said.

"Mrs. Brown called your mother at six this morning and said Mouse wasn't home yet." Dad spoke from behind the newspaper, and all I could see of him was his legs from the knees down.

"As we were walking home, Mouse got into a car with somebody named Bob," I said.

"Morris Brown is headed for trouble," said Mother. It took me a second to figure out who she meant, for

Mouse is seldom called by his real name. "Just wait and see. Harold, I don't think Thomas should go around with Morris Brown."

Dad cleared his throat and turned a page.

"Harold, will you put that paper down and look at me?"

He lowered the paper and looked at her.

"Harold, I don't think Thomas should go around with Morris Brown."

"Nonsense. Tom knows right from wrong." He disappeared behind the paper again.

"But Morris Brown is a bad influence."

Dad turned a page and said nothing.

"What did Chad and Gert have to say?" I asked, hoping to change the subject.

"The letter was mostly about a trip they plan to take in September," said Mother. "They're going to North Dakota for a wedding on Labor Day weekend."

"Whose wedding?"

"Somebody on Gert's side of the family. Somebody we've never met."

I finished my toast and started on the caramel rolls.

"They were hoping you could come up and watch the resort for them while they're away. But I'm writing to say you have a full-time job this summer."

I nodded, regretting for the first time my full-time job. What a great weekend that would be. I would take the bus to Pinecone, and I would have the run of Uncle Chad's place for three days. I would fish for walleyed pike in the morning and evening, and I would swim during the heat of the day. I would wander the trails that wound through the woods and get that feeling again of being completely on my own, away from everyone else in the world.

Each day when I'd been up there before, I used to walk away from Uncle Chad's place and try to pick my way through a part of the forest I hadn't see before. Getting lost never really worried me because Leaf Lake is big. If I used the sun as my compass I was sure to come out somewhere along the shoreline. I often discovered meadows with abandoned farmhouses or cabins, and I realized that no matter how loud I might call, no one in the world could possibly hear me. That's when I would turn back. It's nice to get away from the human race—but only for a while. It was always nice to get back among people in time for supper.

"Harold, don't you think life might be easier if we lived in the country like Chad and Gert?" Mother was folding the letter she had written and looking at it as though she wanted to follow it to Pinecone.

Dad mumbled. We could feel him frowning through the newspaper.

"I'm thinking of the peace and quiet of the lake country," Mother said. "And the cool evenings. You know, Harold, sometimes during hot weather like this I think—"

Dad lowered the paper in a noisy crumple. She started over again, from a different angle.

"Up among the woods and lakes there isn't so much trouble for a teenager to get into. Temptations, I mean."

"There isn't any money to be made either," Dad said, and he went on to list a lot of other things the north country didn't have: major league baseball, five television channels, buses, civilization—he counted them on his fingers until a breeze came along and blew the sports page off his lap.

"But, Harold, you know as well as I do—"

Dad chased the paper to the parapet and trapped a sheet with his foot. He watched another sheet sail down to the street below, then he returned and ended the conversation:

"The north country is there for anybody that wants to move there and live like a peasant. Now I'll say good-day. It's past my bedtime."

Mother and Dad went down to the apartment, and I hurried off to work.

Chapter 7

I got to the store a few minutes late. The door was locked. I walked around to the alley and climbed the outside stairway and knocked on Mr. Kerr's door. No answer. I noticed his car was gone. I went down and sat on the bottom step. A half hour later he came driving down the alley.

"Where have you been?" I asked. "It's eight thirty."

"I know what time it is." He got out of the car and opened the trunk. "Look here," he said.

Lying across the spare tire was a northern pike. It wasn't the biggest northern I had ever seen—it was about a twelve-pounder, and I had once seen a seventeen-pounder caught in Leaf Lake—but it was the biggest fish I had ever seen in St. Paul. It had a broad head, with a mouth big enough to put your fist into. There was a slight movement in its gills. I touched its dull green side, and it flipped itself out of the trunk with a sudden effort and dropped to the ground at our feet, curling its tail around first to one side, then to the other. We waited till it appeared drained of energy, then Mr. Kerr bent over and picked it up by its eye sockets. He held it waist-high and the trail dragged on the ground as he carried it into the store.

"Where did you get him?" I asked.

"In the Mississippi, below the power dam. Fished from shore. Get the lettuce and berries out of the cooler, boy. Make up for lost time."

As I worked at the fruit and vegetable rack, Mr. Kerr laid the fish on the chopping block behind the meat counter and went to get his lettuce-trimming knife from the back room. When he returned he found the fish on the floor trying to curl itself into a circle. He picked up the crowbar we use for opening crates and rapped the fish on the head. It went limp. He picked it up and put it back on the table. He wasn't certain how to begin cleaning it. His breath whistled heavily through his nose and he circled the table with his knife.

I unlocked the front door and let in the old man who comes every morning to buy day-old rolls. Mr. Kerr showed the old man the fish, and between the two of them they butchered it. I mean, they really butchered it. When they got done—and it took them over an hour—the edible parts couldn't have weighed more than two pounds.

The old man bought his half-dozen day-old rolls and was about to leave when Mr. Kerr called him back.

"Let me tell you how I caught this fish," he said, rubbing his hands together. I know how he felt. I know from experience that the only thing better than catching a big fish is telling people about it.

"I caught it in the Mississippi below the power dam."

"I know the place," said the old man. "Never fished there myself, though. Never was much of a hand to fish."

"Well, you know where that point of land juts out into the water? That's where I fish." Mr. Kerr took up his story-telling position, one arm draped over the cash register and the other hand under his apron, scratching his stomach. "I got out there at five thirty when it was just getting light in the east."

"Five thirty in the morning?" I said.

"Of course."

"I didn't know anybody got up at that hour."

"I often get up at that hour in the summer. I don't sleep so good in the heat. My apartment's like an oven."

"Get on with how you caught the fish," said the old man, sitting down on a box of apples. He loved being talked to.

"Well, sir, I rigged up a strong leader and a hook with a big minnow on it, and I put two heavy sinkers on the line so the current wouldn't take it down-stream, then I put on a sliding bobber and threw the whole mess into the water. Then I sat down and watched the sun come up and the gulls fly around and I thought, This is the life. What am I doing cooped up in a grocery store all day when I could be fishing? Right then and there I came to a decision. Before another year passes I'm putting this store up for sale, and a year from today—what is it? June 16?—I'm going to be fishing out of a boat somewhere in the north woods. Next year on June 16 you might be sitting here bruising a boxful of apples, but they won't be my apples, and you won't see me anywhere around."

In order to remain within earshot, I had been dusting the cans in the front window, though I had just put them there the day before and they didn't need dusting.

"Are you serious, Mr. Kerr?" I asked. I had planned to work for Mr. Kerr at least until I graduated—if I ever graduated—if not longer.

"You heard me, boy."

"You mean you might sell the store?"

"Within a year's time. You can count on it."

"Get on with how you caught the fish," said the old man.

"Well, I fell asleep," said Mr. Kerr. "There's a mist around the power dam that cools off the air and makes it comfortable for sleeping early in the morning. I got sleepy watching the bobber. I laid right down on the ground with my arm over my eyes and fell asleep. I slept for an hour and a half. Couldn't believe it when I woke up and looked at my watch. I looked for my bobber. It was gone. Something had taken it under. I

36

grabbed for my rod and reel, but my rod and reel weren't where I left them. My rod and reel were inching down the bank toward the water. I ran to the edge of the water in time to grab them and I felt a tremendous tug on the line."

Mr. Kerr clenched his fists together, as though he were gripping a rod and straining to land a big fish.

"I pulled on the rod and the fish headed out for the middle of the river. I couldn't turn him around. I just gave him line and let him go. That was all I could do. It's a wonder he didn't wind my line around something and snap it in two, there's a lot of junk in the river. It took me twenty minutes to land him. I would reel in a little line, then he'd take off again. But little by little I gained on him. When I got him up in the shallows, he got mad and jumped clear out of the water and twisted around like a pretzel. That's when I saw how big he was."

Mr. Kerr was working up a sweat. He finished the demonstration by backing down the soup and vegetable aisle in short jerky steps to show how he had dragged the fish up on the sand.

"There he lay," said Mr. Kerr, breathing strenuously through his nose. "The biggest fish I ever saw." He looked at us to see how we were reacting.

I nodded to show him I was impressed.

The old man on the apple box was asleep.

"Mr. Kerr," I said, "if you sell the store, I'll be out of a job."

"No. If you want to stay, you can work for the next owner. But you won't want to stay. Another year, and you'll want to try some other line of work. There's better lines of work than stocking shelves. That was quite a fish, wasn't it?"

"Yes, it was. But I don't know if I'd like another line of work. I like working here."

"You've been a good right-hand man for me, boy. A little careless with the lettuce sometimes. A little careless giving change a time or two. But you're honest. Honesty is a great virtue. As long as you're honest, you haven't got a thing to worry about. I'll write you a recommendation that will get you a job wherever you want. You can't spend your life working for me. I'm old and ready to take it easy. I'm going to find me a shack in the north woods beside a lake and stay year-round: summers, fish in a boat; winters, fish through the ice. Wasn't that some fish I caught this morning?"

"Some fish, all right. But up at my Uncle Chad's place I've seen northerns bigger than that. And walleyes up to six or eight pounds."

"Where's that?"

"Up on Leaf Lake. Near Pinecone. My Uncle Chad's got a resort up there."

"That's the kind of place I'm talking about. The area around Pinecone. A fisherman's paradise. When I find a place to live up there, you can take a few days off and come up and fish with me."

The old man on the box of apples began to snore, and Mr. Kerr tapped him on the shoulder.

"Get on with the story of how you caught the fish," the old man said.

"It's over. I've told it, and you slept through it."

The old man shook his head and stretched and stood up and left the store with his little sack of day-old rolls.

Chapter 8

That night at closing time I was in the basement sorting pop bottles. Mr. Kerr locked the front door and counted the money from the cash register and put it in a bag and carried it to his desk in the back room. He turned off most of the lights and called down the stairs, "It's quitting time."

"I'll be done in a minute," I said. "There's a few more bottles to sort."

A minute later, above the clink of bottles, I thought I heard a commotion upstairs. I stopped sorting and listened. Somebody was rattling the front door. I heard Mr. Kerr shove his chair away from his desk and walk to the front of the store. I had an uneasy feeling. I climbed the stairs and stood looking out toward the front. The store was dark except for the lamp over Mr.

Kerr's desk and the dim light shining up from the basement.

I heard Mr. Kerr say, "Store's closed."

"Please, Mr. Kerr, my mother needs some aspirin bad." I didn't recognize the voice that came through the glass.

I heard Mr. Kerr turn his key in the lock.

The door swung open with such force the glass shattered to the floor.

The same voice said, "I'll sit on the old man. Get busy."

I stayed in the shadows of the back room. I could see a figure moving around the check-out counter. He was rattling a paper sack and filling it with something—probably cartons of cigarettes, which we kept in a drawer under the cash register. It couldn't have been money, because the bag of money was on Mr. Kerr's desk. I tiptoed over to the desk, picked up the bag, and switched off the desk lamp. In the faint light shining up from the basement I was able to find my way back to the head of the basement stairs without bumping into anything. The basement light switch was at the head of the stairs. I switched it off, then in total darkness I felt my way down, step by step.

The blood was beating so hard in my ears, it was a few seconds before I could hear anything. Then I heard the sound of scuffling near the front door and footsteps approaching the back room.

I slipped the money under the bottom step and felt around for a weapon. I picked up a large Coke bottle and, carrying it like a club, I started up the steps again. I didn't want to be trapped in the basement.

When I got to the top, I could hear someone at the far end of the back room near Mr. Kerr's desk rummaging around, bumping into things, and knocking account books and pencils onto the floor.

The scuffling sound died near the front door, and a voice called, "Mouse, where are you?" It was the same voice that asked for the aspirin.

The figure standing over Mr. Kerr's desk said, "Looking for the bag of money." It was Mouse's voice.

"You've got to hurry. Somebody's going to walk by and see this door busted open."

"Listen, just keep the old man quiet. I'll be with you in a minute," said Mouse.

"Don't worry about the old man. He's out cold."

I pressed myself against the wall at the head of the stairs. I felt for the basement light switch. I turned on the basement light.

Mouse whirled around. He thought someone was in the basement, and he hurried over to the top of the steps. He stood in front of me, peering down into the light. This was my chance. He wasn't more than two feet away. I swung the bottle at his head. I didn't land a good blow, but it was enough to knock him off balance, and he tumbled backward down the steps, shouting as he went.

I ran to the front of the store and found Mr. Kerr lying by the door, but his assailant was gone. He had heard the shout and beat it.

I ran into the street and stopped a passing car. In a few seconds ten or twelve people gathered in front of the store. A big man in Bermuda shorts snatched away the Coke bottle (which I hadn't realized I was still carrying) and he pinned my arms behind my back.

"Call the police," he hollered. "I've got the thief."

"Let me go," I said. "I work here."

"Tell it to the police."

Someone recognized Mr. Kerr in the doorway. "That's Henry Kerr. He's been beat up. The kid must have beat him with that pop bottle."

"Let me go!" I said.

But the man in Bermuda shorts would not release me. "We're keeping everything as is," he said, "so the cops can see how it happened."

"But I work here. We've just been robbed."

It was no use.

By the time a squad car arrived, Mr. Kerr had crawled out onto the sidewalk and collapsed and lay silently at my feet. I was afraid he was dead. He looked dead. A great crowd was milling around. Someone had gone into the store and turned on the lights. Through the window I saw a man taking cans off a shelf and putting them in a sack.

Two patrolmen got out of the car, and one of them said, "What happened? Who saw it happen?"

"I did," I said. "I work for Mr. Kerr, and I can't get my arms loose."

"Release him," said the patrolman.

The man in shorts released me. "We found him leaving the store with this bottle," he said. With his foot he nudged the bottle on the sidewalk.

"What's your name?" the patrolman asked me.

"Tom Barry," I said. "Two men broke into the store."

"What's your middle name?"

"Edward."

"Now tell me what happened."

The man who had held me spoke up. "Don't let him talk his way out of it," he said. "We saw him come running out of the store."

"Look," I said, "if I was a robber, would I be wearing this apron?"

Everybody looked at me. I forgot. I had taken my apron off before I went into the basement to sort bottles.

An ambulance and another squad car drove up.

"You can tell your story to Mr. Afton," said the patrolman. He put me in his car and drove off to the police station on Marshall Avenue.

At the station I sat on a bench for several minutes, under the watchful eye of the desk sergeant. Then a man I recognized came up and introduced himself. He was the man who stopped at the store every morning for two packs of Winstons. I hadn't known he was a detective.

"My name's Afton," he said. "Aren't you the fellow who sells me cigarettes?"

"That's right," I said. "You don't think I'm a suspect, do you?"

"Not at all, not at all. You're Mr. Kerr's right-hand man. Let's see, it says here," he looked at his clipboard, "it says here Tom Barry. Nice to meet you, Tom. Come down the hall with me and we'll have a chat."

He led me into a quiet room, where he had me speak

into a tape recorder. I told almost everything I could remember. When I got to the part about hiding the bag of money, he picked up the phone and told the desk sergeant to radio the men at the store. He said they should look under the bottom step in the basement. In a few seconds the desk sergeant reported that they found the bag of money.

"Did they catch anyone in the store?" I asked. "I think one of the men was still in there when I ran out the front."

"No sign of him. Both men made a clean getaway."

"He must have gone out the back door. Mr. Kerr doesn't lock it till he goes upstairs to bed."

"That's what happened, no doubt."

"What about Mr. Kerr? Is he alive?"

"No word from the hospital yet. We'll hear from the doctor shortly. Now, Tom, the question is, who were those two men?"

"I wish I knew. I hate to think of them running loose, especially after what they did to Mr. Kerr."

"How much could you see of them?"

"All I could see was the silhouette of the man I pushed downstairs. He was between me and the basement light. He was a little shorter than I am. That's all I know."

This was a lie. I knew it was Mouse.

"Their voices, Tom. Think hard about their voices. Were they voices you ever heard before? And did they call each other by name?"

"I don't remember."

"Don't answer right away. Think back. Take your time. What did they say? What did they sound like?"

I looked at the floor and shook my head.

"You don't remember?"

"No," I said.

"You heard no names?"

"No."

"What about their voices? Was there anything familiar about their voices?"

I shook my head.

"I'm surprised," he said.

"Why?"

"Because it was a job done by someone familiar with the store. Someone you might have waited on a few times. At least one of them knew where the cigarettes were kept. And knew the best time to strike. And was able to find his way back to Mr. Kerr's desk."

"No," I said, "I didn't recognize the voices."

There was a long, uncomfortable pause. I was having trouble looking Mr. Afton in the eye.

Then the phone rang. It was a report from General Hospital. Mr. Kerr had a fractured skull and a separated shoulder. His condition was serious, but he would recover.

"That's a relief," I said.

"Yes, to you and me both," said Mr. Afton. "And to his assailant, whoever he is. At least he won't have a homicide charge against him."

"And the store," I said. "What about the store?"

"Don't worry about it. We're locking it and boarding up the glass door."

"I'm out of a job then."

"It looks that way. Mr. Kerr won't be well enough to reopen for quite some time."

Mr. Afton took me outside to a squad car parked at the curb. He introduced me to the patrolman and held the door while I got in. He shook my hand through the window and said, "I congratulate you on the way you handled yourself during the break-in, Tom. The way you saved the money."

"I only wish I could have saved Mr. Kerr."

"That was out of the question. You did all that was possible, I'm sure. Now here is what remains for you to do. Two things. First, you're going to be turning this business over in your mind for a few days and nights—especially these hot nights when you're lying in bed and can't sleep. And the more you think about it, the more you'll remember. And when you uncover something in your memory, some clue, anything at all, no matter how small, you will please call me on the phone immediately. Here's a card with my home number and my office number. Call any time of the day or night. I'll be glad to hear from you."

"O.K., Mr. Afton."

"And second, we'll need you to identify suspects when we round them up. We'll call you down here to point your finger."

"O.K., I'll do my best. But it was pretty dark. I'm not sure I can be much help."

"Your best is all we ask."

We shook hands again and the patrolman drove me home.

Mr. Afton had phoned Mother and Dad, and they were waiting for me on the sidewalk outside the apartment house. Dad beamed when I told the story of the robbery. He especially liked the part where I pushed one of the men down the basement stairs. He said it was a heroic thing to do. He took me to several apartments to tell the story to the neighbors, until Mother finally convinced him it was time we were all in bed.

I couldn't sleep. My mind raced back and forth over the events of the evening, and I became more and more dissatisfied with myself. Instead of hanging back in the shadows, I should have run to the front and defended Mr. Kerr. Was I scared? Did I think the bag of money was worth more than Mr. Kerr's life?

But if I had run to his aid, we both might have been beaten up, maybe even killed, if they'd had a gun. Who knows what might have happened? Right or wrong, it was too late now to change what I'd done.

But it wasn't too late yet to tell the police about Mouse. Mr. Afton said I could call him any time. Was I certain it was Mouse? It was Mouse, all right. His summer job was robbing stores. That's what he'd meant by night work. That's why he was running around with Bob What's-his-name, the ex-con. That's why he'd come into the store last night and watched us count the money. That's why he'd asked me which days were busiest and where the money was hidden overnight. He'd been sent by Bob to find out that information.

I almost got out of bed and went to the phone, but instead I tried to think of reasons not to. I thought of several. Is a guy supposed to squeal on his best friend? Was it my responsibility to send Mouse Brown to the reformatory? They say the reformatory is where young lawbreakers are turned into hardened criminals. Hadn't I done enough? Wasn't it the job of the police to find the guilty? If the trail led to Mouse, that was police business. Not mine.

And what about Mouse's family? It wasn't very stable. His two younger brothers looked up to him as an example. His mother was a nervous wreck. His father was kind of unbalanced. The family might fall apart if they found out what Mouse was up to.

What was he up to? Was I certain of his guilt? Had I actually seen him in the store? In the dark? I had only heard someone say, "Mouse." How many Mouses were there in St. Paul? Certainly he wasn't the only one.

No money was stolen. And Mr. Kerr would recover. And the glass in the front door would be replaced. We lost more to shoplifters than we did to robbers.

All these reasons satisfied me for a while, and I dropped into a kind of half-sleep with my eyes half-open. I don't know how long I lay like that—a couple of minutes, a couple of hours—then the image of Mr. Kerr gradually began to take shape in my mind. I saw him lying at my feet like a corpse, his head bloody.

I got out of bed and went to the kitchen to use the phone. I would call Mr. Afton.

But I found Mother and Dad sitting at the table drinking wine and arguing. So I opened a can of pop and joined them.

"What's the city coming to?" Mother was saying. "A boy can't work at an honest job without risking his

JON HASSLER

life? The city is not a fit place for decent people. It's full of thieves and robbers."

"Now, Margaret."

"Just last week Hilda Jennings' milk was stolen from her front doorstep two days in a row. I told you, Harold, when we first moved to the city—"

"I know what you told me, Margaret."

"If we had stayed in the north country and lived among decent, law-abiding country people, we wouldn't be putting Thomas through this suffering."

"Who's suffering? Thomas isn't suffering. He's proving himself a man. Besides, there's as many law-breakers in the country as there are in the city."

"That's not so. Nine out of ten lawbreakers live in cities. Whoever heard about crime like this in the country?"

"Margaret, don't you see there's more crime in the city because there're more people in the city? Crime is the same everywhere, in proportion to the population. If there are fewer bad people in the country, there are fewer good people too."

"Hear that?" said Mother. "There's a siren on Marshall Avenue right now."

It was the same argument I had heard a dozen times, and it never seemed to get them anywhere. Neither of them convinced the other. I was inclined to agree with Mother. From my vacations on Leaf Lake I got the impression that country people led lives of total peace and quiet, never a disturbance. But, on the other hand, I could see Dad's point. If a man's principles were strong enough he could live anywhere and not turn rotten.

50

Dad changed the subject. "Has it occurred to you, Thomas, that you may be out of work?"

"Maybe for a while," I said. "Until Mr. Kerr recovers."

"Maybe for good. Henry Kerr's no spring chicken. He'll be a long time recovering. He's an old bachelor with a pile of money and it wouldn't surprise me if he sold out and retired."

"It's possible," I said. "Just this morning he talked about retiring next year."

"There you are."

"But he said I can probably work for the new owner."

"Maybe you can and maybe you can't. That store is a one-man operation. Or say a husband-and-wife team bought it—they could handle the business without your help."

"I suppose they could. But if I'm out of work, what do I do for money? It's too late to find another job for the summer."

"That's what I was leading up to. How much money have you got now?"

"A couple hundred dollars. Not bad, but I doubt if it will last me through the next school year. Buying clothes and everything. Don't forget, I gave you half of everything I made."

"I know you did. And here it is." He pulled a savings account book out of the kitchen drawer where he keeps his papers, and he handed it to me.

"What's this?" I asked. The account book had my name on it.

"That's half your pay over the last year, plus interest. I've been putting it in the bank for you. It's yours."

What a fantastic thing for him to do. I didn't know what to say.

"But that doesn't solve his job problem for the summer," said Mother. "He can't just be roaming the streets."

"Margaret, I swear, when you get to heaven the first thing you'll do is look for something to worry about."

"It's one o'clock," said Mother. "I'm going back to bed. And tomorrow I'll write another letter to Chad and Gert. I'll tell them Thomas will be up for the Labor Day weekend, after all."

"That will be fine with me," I said. "And thank you for the bank account."

"Don't mention it," said Dad. "Just be careful how you spend the money."

"And be careful how you spend the summer," said Mother.

I went to bed without calling Mr. Afton. I was suddenly very tired. Morning would be soon enough.

Chapter 9

I woke up at seven and ate breakfast and left the apartment. I didn't want Mother listening to my phone call. I went to the pay phone on the corner, but instead of calling Mr. Afton, I called Mouse. I'm not sure why. Maybe I expected that hearing his voice would confirm my suspicions.

"Hello."

"Hello. Mouse?"

"Yeah. Who's this?"

"It's me. Tom."

"Yeah? What do you want? You got me out of bed."

"I just wanted to know if you've started on my story."

"What story?"

"My story for Mr. Singleton. Forty-seven pages."

"Listen, I haven't had time. Keep your shirt on, will you?"

"Well, I just wanted to say don't start on it till I tell you. I might have time to write it myself. I might be out of a job."

"No kidding? How come?" He sounded surprised.

"It's a long story I'll tell you some other time."

"O.K., but not so early in the morning. I'm going back to bed."

"O.K. So long."

"So long."

If he had sounded guilty, nervous, scared, or flustered, I would have called the police. But he only sounded sleepy.

I walked to the grocery store and found that the door had been boarded up and there was a closed sign in the window.

From there I got a bus to General Hospital and asked the girl at the desk if I could see Mr. Kerr.

"You aren't family, are you?"

"Not really," I said, "but I'm all the family he's got. I work for him in his store."

"All right, you may see him for a minute. Room 704. But you mustn't be long."

I found my way up to 704, and there, lying in a bed with rails around it, was Mr. Kerr with his head and shoulder bandaged. He was drugged and weak, but he tried to squeeze my hand.

"They tell me you came out of it without a scratch," he said. His tongue was thick.

I nodded.

"And they tell me you hid the money."

"That's right. But I wished I'd have helped you out instead."

"It wouldn't have done any good. I got clubbed and you would have got clubbed too."

"How are you feeling?"

"I'm not running the hundred-yard dash."

"What about the store, Mr. Kerr?"

"My grocery days are over. I'm selling out. I've already had the nurse call a realtor this morning."

There was a long pause. We didn't look at each other.

Finally I said, "I'll keep my eye on the place for you."

"Yes, you'll have to do that. On your way out, stop at the nurse's station and pick up my key ring. Then you can let the realtor into the store when he brings someone around. He has your name and address. And you might as well use my car while I'm in here. And bring me my mail every day. I'll keep you on salary till I'm up and around."

"That's not necessary. I'll do it for nothing. I've got money saved up."

"We'll see. I'm in no shape to argue today. My headache's coming back." He pressed the button for the nurse. "Come back tomorrow." He closed his eyes. "Thank God you didn't get clubbed," he said.

A nurse hurried in and gave me a dirty look and shooed me out of the room. From another nurse I got Mr. Kerr's key ring. I took a bus back to the store and drove home in his car.

With Mr. Kerr directing me from his hospital bed, I was busy for a long time. He had me dispose of the perishable goods—the milk, the meat, the fruit, and fresh vegetables—by giving them away to charitable institutions. I called places like the Bethany Rest Home, and St. Patrick's Orphanage, and the Salvation Army, and I delivered whatever they could use. Then he had me empty the refrigerators and the freezer and disconnect them and give the ice cream, butter and cheese to whoever looked like they needed it in the neighborhood. Then, with Dad's help, I replaced the glass in the door. I kept everything dusted, so the store would look more appealing to the prospective buyers that showed up now and then with the realtor.

Time passed and I never got a call from the police station.

In mid-July the store was sold to a pizza-maker. He brought in a team of carpenters and began turning it into a pizza parlor, and I spent several days taking the stock off the shelves and packing it in boxes and selling it back to the jobbers. Whatever I didn't know what to do with—shelving, furniture, light fixtures—I carried upstairs to Mr. Kerr's apartment. The pizza-maker had said he could live there until the end of September.

When Mr. Kerr came home at the end of July, his apartment looked like a junk shop, and it was mid-August before we got it cleaned out. Mr. Kerr got on the phone and called around to antique dealers and junkmen and cabinetmakers, and I drove here and there, dropping things off and collecting the few dollars he got for it all. Besides selling the store fixtures, Mr. Kerr sold most of the furniture in his apartment. He was determined to find himself a cabin in the north woods and sent for real-estate brochures. We studied them by the hour, but everything listed for sale was pretty fancy. He wanted only a one- or two-room cabin, and the realtors didn't seem to be dealing in anything as small as that.

The summer passed in a series of heat waves and thunderstorms. I played some pool and did some swimming at the Y. I went to Met Stadium with Dad a few times and watched the Twins get dumped. Now and then Mr. Kerr and I would go down to the power dam and catch a few bullheads.

As time went by I began to wonder how Mr. Kerr would manage all by himself in the north woods. His strength was not coming back as fast as I'd expected, and his left arm was nearly useless. When he was tired, he got severe headaches. When I watched him climb the stairs to his apartment and almost collapse from exhaustion, or when I saw him fumble with his shoestrings or his can opener—whatever took two hands—I was tempted to call Mr. Afton and report Mouse Brown.

Chapter 10

But Mouse was having problems of his own.

One day when I came home for supper, Mother said, "Have you heard the news?"

"No," I said. "What happened?"

"Mr. Brown jumped off the Tenth Avenue bridge."

"Mouse's dad? Into the Mississippi?"

"Yes, and he lived through it. Mrs. Brown called me. She said he's in General Hospital. The mental ward."

I didn't see Mouse after that until the end of August, when we met one day in Tilbury's Cafe. I asked him how his dad was getting along.

"Dad's as good as ever—so-so."

"But I heard he tried to kill himself."

"It was a half-hearted try," said Mouse. "For weeks

before it happened, he was silent as a statue. If any of us tried to strike up a conversation with him, he'd pretend to be interested in a magazine or he'd get up and move to another room. Then I started bringing money home from my summer job [he still wouldn't admit what he was doing for the summer]. Listen, I was helping to pay for the groceries and for my kid brothers' clothes. In July I even paid the rent. When I first started this job, I was planning to keep the money all for me. But the more I thought about it, the more I could see that Ma needed the money for the family. Besides, I was making so much I couldn't spend it all," he said. "And that's when Dad started acting strange—when I brought home money."

"How do you know that's what did it?" I asked.

"Well, he never was much of a talker," said Mouse. "But he'd always been pretty well satisfied to sit around and drink beer and mind his own business. He would crack a joke once in a while and listen to Ma's gossip. Ma knows more about the neighbors than the neighbors do. She's on the phone all the time. And he would put in a day or two working for the street department when they needed extra help. You know he never said much—he was easygoing.

"But one day while we were eating supper and Ma was explaining to Rickie why we couldn't afford a new pair of tennis shoes, I took forty dollars out of my pocket and laid it down in the middle of the table. It was my first experience at being a big charity man, and I wanted to be dramatic. So right when Ma said, 'We never have enough money,' I whipped out the four bills and put them down with such a flourish I knocked over the catsup.

"The kids got excited, and Ma snatched up the money and put it in her pocket. But Dad never said a word. He never said 'Thank you,' 'Where did you get it?' or 'Put it back in your pocket.' He just got up and left the table."

"Didn't he care where you got the money?" I asked, hoping someone would get on to Mouse besides me.

"Who could tell?" said Mouse. "So I said to myself, 'He'll get used to it.' I never knew anyone yet who could turn down money handed to them on a platter. So I gave them another forty dollars the next week, only I didn't make a big production out of it. I simply handed the money to Ma when I knew Dad was looking, and I said, 'Here's another forty dollars, and the kids don't have to know I gave it to you.'

"But it didn't make any difference. Dad still acted as though his favorite brewery had burned down. I guess he was mad to think I was making more money than he was. So for a while I quit my contributions—my income isn't all that steady anyhow— and Dad looked like he was about to perk up. But Ma told me that if I didn't continue to do my part we would have to go back to eating sardines. With my money she had been buying TV dinners that you put in the oven and eat out of the package. After a couple weeks of those I was ready for sardines any day. You know what I mean, don't you? Those frozen dinners? You wrestle with all that cardboard and plastic and tinfoil, and then you find that the applesauce has spilled over into the string bean compartment."

"Yeah, I know," I said. "Mother gets them once in a while. You should hear my dad kick. Well, what did you do then?"

"Ma said if I didn't pitch in with some cash the little boys would have to go around in ragged clothes. So I pitched in and did my share, and the next thing we knew the police called to say they had taken the old man to the hospital. They said he had tried to kill himself by jumping into the river, and would Ma please come down and explain what was going on."

"What did she say?" I asked.

"What did Ma know! She fell apart. I had to go with her on the bus to make sure she got to the hospital, and she talked nonsense all the way across town.

"Once we got there, I figured it would be simply a matter of checking him out—like picking up a suit at the dry cleaners. But no, they were drying him off in the psychiatric ward and they weren't very anxious to turn him loose. In fact, on that first day we never got to see him at all. We were put in a little room with a man in a cowboy shirt who asked us a lot of personal questions and a woman who answered them before Ma or I could open our mouths. I know a wig-picker when I see one, and even though he didn't introduce himself I knew the cowboy was a psychiatrist.

"We knew the woman. She's a social worker who turns up snooping around our apartment every few months. The welfare office sends her around to their clients. She's no prize. She's one of those short women who have the knack of looking down their noses at you until you feel shorter than they are. You know the type—stiff and proper all the time and looking as though they smelled something bad. Well, she's one of those. The four of us sat in a circle around a table in this tiny room with no windows and nothing on the walls except a picture of a horse.

"The psychiatrist came out with a steady stream of questions for at least ten minutes. Not the normal kind of questions you might expect like where do you live? And what's eating your old man? He asked odd questions like how many people sleep in each bed in our apartment? And are the kids allowed to walk around naked? The social worker answered for us. She spat out the answers as fast as he could jot them down. She was wrong about half the time, but we let her go ahead because Ma and I both had shaky voices. When the questions were over, the cowboy said, 'Come back tomorrow at noon and you can visit Mr. Brown.'"

"How many days did they keep him in the hospital?" I asked.

"Six days. We were a little nervous at first, wondering if being kept there like a prisoner would make him angry, but it wasn't half bad. We came to see him every day, and he would be up and dressed and walking around the halls or maybe he would be in the game room playing pool with some other patients. It didn't seem right to Ma that a hospital patient should be having a good time, and she asked him one day, 'Don't you think you're ready to come home?' And Dad said, 'A change of scenery is good for a guy once in a while.'

"We saw the psychiatrist that day too—he was wearing a purple cowboy shirt with orange piping. And Ma said it was high time the old man came home, and the psychiatrist said, 'Give him another day or two. He's enjoying the change of scenery.' Then he said something that sounded ridiculous. He said, 'After all, that's what Mr. Brown was looking for under the Tenth Avenue bridge—a change of scenery.'"

Mouse paused to let me think that over.

"Sounds ridiculous, all right," I said.

"Only at first. If you think about it for a while and if you can forget you heard it from someone in a purple cowboy shirt, it starts making sense."

"Maybe so," I said.

"Anyhow, Dad's been home two weeks and he's like he used to be—lazy. But at least he speaks when he's spoken to, which is more than he did during those bad weeks. I think that business under the bridge did him good. He went out and had his little adventure and now he's satisfied, and I don't look for him to do it again. I think it scared him. He didn't jump from very high up, but the dive scared him all the same."

"Does he ever talk about what he did?"

"He never mentions it. And we don't bring it up. That little shrimp of a social worker came over one day and wanted to talk about it, but the old man told her to get lost. She's been back twice since then, and she keeps quiet. She just snoops around the cupboards and the closets. She's one of the benefits you get when you're on welfare."

"Do you still give your folks money?"

"Now and then I give Ma a bill or two, but I tell her to lay off the frozen dinners."

"It sounds like you're head of the family."

"I guess I am. My old man and my old lady and my brothers are depending on me. Which is O.K. My income is good."

"How do you earn it?"

Mouse gave me a sly look. Then he said, "Listen, Tom, what are you doing Labor Day weekend?"

"I'm going north to my uncle's place."

"That's no fun. Why don't you come with me and Bob Peabody?"

"Bob Peabody?"

"Yeah. My business partner. We're driving to Madison, Wisconsin, for the big Labor Day races. Three days of racing. There's going to be a crowd of twenty-five thousand. It's a great place to meet girls."

"Sorry, I've already got my ticket to Pinecone. My bus leaves at noon on Friday."

Chapter 11

I was the only passenger to get off the bus in
Pinecone. Uncle Chad shook my hand while Aunt Gert
squeezed my arm and told me I was growing too fast.
They both called me Tommy.

The three of us climbed into Uncle Chad's pickup
and drove north out of town. After we had gone about
four miles on the highway, we came to a sign that said
CHAD'S CABINS, and we turned onto a dirt road
that dipped and rose through a thick pine forest. The
sun hadn't set yet, but the trees were so thick and
close to the road it was like driving through a tunnel,
and Uncle Chad had to turn on his headlights.

"There's nobody staying in the cabins this weekend," he said. "We didn't take any reservations
because of the wedding we have to go to. So all you do

65

is turn people away if they come looking for a place to stay. Gert don't want to come home to a bundle of dirty bedsheets."

"Oh, hush," said Aunt Gert, sitting between us. "You know very well we had no reservations in the first place. You needn't lie about your business to Tommy like you do to your resorter friends. Tommy's your nephew."

"All right, Gert."

"Labor Day weekend is never very busy around here," said Aunt Gert. "It's too chilly this far north."

We drove over a hill I remembered from previous summers. The lake lay before us, orange in the sunset.

"The lake is even prettier than I remember it," I said.

"You bet it's pretty," said Uncle Chad. "And that ain't all. Leaf Lake has the clearest water south of Canada. The bottom is all clean sand, and the walleyes are so thick you get sick of catching them. Besides that, the nights are cool."

Just over the hill the road divided into two narrow driveways. I knew the one on the left was Uncle Chad's, but he took the one on the right.

"We'll drop in on Lester Flett for a minute," he said, "and let you get reacquainted."

I recalled that Lester Flett, who lived in a little cabin at the edge of Uncle Chad's property, used to hire out as a fishing guide. It was said that he was once a newspaper reporter in Minneapolis, but he turned his back on civilization and lived like a hermit.

"Is Lester still a fishing guide?" I asked.

"No, he doesn't do much guiding any more," said Uncle Chad. "Fact is, he doesn't do much of anything. He's generally what you might call a brush rabbit."

"Now, Chad, he's a friend of ours," said Aunt Gert. "Don't call him a brush rabbit. He's over for coffee almost every day, and he's as friendly and polite as he can be."

"I never said he wasn't friendly and polite. Brush rabbits are generally friendly and polite. Especially when there's some bread and jam goes with the coffee. A man like Lester Flett who lives off the land learns to take his nourishment wherever he can get it. If it ain't bread and jam at the neighbors', it's walleyes when they're biting, and venison out of season."

"You mean he poaches?" I asked.

"He poaches like a wolf poaches. When he needs to. As long as he eats all the meat he kills, I guess it goes for a good cause. It keeps a man alive. Nothing so criminal about that."

We drove over a rough spot in the narrow driveway, and our headlights jumped up and down on the wall of an old shed that stood facing us in a clearing. The driveway curved around and stopped between the shed and a small cabin.

"He's home," said Aunt Gert. "I see a light inside. But we can't stay long. We're getting up early in the morning."

Lester Flett came to the door, barefoot. He was smaller than I remembered him. He came up to my shoulder. His face was dark and wrinkled like an old leather glove.

"Come in, come in," he said. "Find a place to sit and I'll serve you up some chokecherry wine. Is this your brother's boy?"

"Yup. My brother's boy," said Uncle Chad. "His name is Tommy."

"Tom," I said.

"He's going to be a junior in high school this year. You probably remember him from past summers."

"You bet I do," said Lester. "So you're leaving him in charge of your place for the weekend, eh?"

"That's right," said Uncle Chad.

We sat down around Lester's table. Uncle Chad sat on a wooden box, Aunt Gert on a rocking chair, and I on a stool. Lester opened an old-fashioned icebox—the kind actually cooled by chunks of ice—and brought out a wine bottle.

He said to me, "You won't have much to do, managing Chad's place this late in the season. Tell you what. I'm going out for walleyes at six tomorrow morning. If you want to go along be down on your dock. I figure the walleyes should be about ready to bite around the sunken island. Have you heard any fishing reports, Chad?"

"Yup, I met a fellow in town this afternoon who had his limit of walleyes at the sunken island. Seems they're biting there, all right."

Lester rummaged through a big dishpan looking for drinking glasses.

"I also met a guy who had his motor stolen last night," said Uncle Chad. "That makes the tenth motor this summer right here on Leaf Lake."

"That's terrible," said Lester, over the clatter of dishes. "I've never seen it so bad for robbery and vandalism. The worst part is that a man can't leave his motor on his boat overnight. Every time I use my motor, I have to lug it back up to the shed. How many motors do you folks have this summer?"

"Four," said Uncle Chad. "One for each cabin. They're all six-horse Mercurys."

"Well, see that you lock them up before you leave tomorrow."

"Don't worry," said Aunt Gert. "Our motors are always locked up when they're not in use. Now you remember that, Tommy. If you take a boat out with a motor on it, put the motor away as soon as you're through with it, and pull the boat all the way up on the sand, so the waves don't take it out again."

Uncle Chad said, "Yes, remember that, Tommy."

"Tom," I said.

Lester gave us each a glass of deep red wine, then he sat on a box that was so low his head barely showed above the table. We all took a sip. Uncle Chad and Aunt Gert said how good it was, and I breathed deep three or four times to cool off my throat.

"Of course, it isn't done fermenting yet," said Lester. "It's this year's crop of chokecherries you're drinking. Chokecherry authorities recommend a lapse of six months between the bush and the belly, but two weeks is good enough for me."

We took another sip.

"How many gallons did you make this year?" asked Uncle Chad.

"Oh, about twenty. I don't know exactly. I had it fermenting all over the cabin in kettles and crocks. It was fun waking up at night and hearing it fizz and bubble."

"Goodness," said Aunt Gert, "twenty gallons takes a lot of sugar."

"You bet it does, Gert."

Uncle Chad said, "If I might ask you a personal question, how were you able to buy enough sugar for twenty gallons of wine?"

"Well, it takes a lot of sugar if you make it with sugar. But me, I make it with honey. I go out and race the bears to the honeycombs."

"Goodness," said Aunt Gert.

I looked around at the cabin. I saw a window on each of the four walls and realized that the small room we sat in was Lester's entire house. It was a real log cabin, with plaster filling up the spaces between the logs. Besides the table and the icebox, he had an old cast-iron stove with a flat top for cooking, two cupboards made out of wooden boxes, a kerosene lamp, and a cot. On one wall was a gun rack containing a rifle and a shotgun.

Sticking out of a wine bottle on the stove was a wild flower—a yellow daisy.

I sipped the wine and it made me warm and sleepy. Only snatches of conversation were getting through to me. Aunt Gert was talking:

"Martha Jones across the lake says the sheriff knows who's stealing the motors. It's a gang of thieves, and he's waiting to get them all in one place and arrest them."

"I doubt if Martha Jones knows anything about it," said Uncle Chad. "A gang of professionals wouldn't take all summer to steal ten motors. If you ask me, it's somebody local, somebody who ain't in a hurry about it, somebody who takes the time to study people's habits. Then he strikes when he's sure he can pick off a motor real easy-like."

Lester said, "I've lived ten years on this lake and I know everybody on it, and I don't believe there's a thief in the whole bunch. That's why I agree with Gert. It must be somebody from the outside. Here, have some more wine."

He filled our glasses. I took a big swallow and my ears started to hum. It was a low buzz that made the voices in the small room sound strange. I decided to try my own voice and see how it sounded.

"You'd think they'd have been caught by this time," I said. I sounded muffled and far away.

"They'll be caught just as soon as they come looking for motors around my place," said Uncle Chad. "And I know just how I'm going to catch them."

"Now, Chad, you be careful," said Aunt Gert.

"If they show up around my place they'll be caught by me personally. [My uncle is like my dad—very sure of himself.] I've heard people talk about these hooligans all summer, and I know their tactics. For one thing, all ten motors have disappeared on windy or rainy nights. That makes sense because hardly anybody else would be on the lake or along the shore on nights like that. When it rains, we're all inside watching TV.

71

"Furthermore, George Anderson claims he seen the fellow that got away with his motor. He says the night his motor disappeared it was raining to beat the band, and he looked out the window and seen this little guy rowing a boat around the bay. It was dusk and he couldn't make out the color of the boat and he couldn't see the guy's face, but he said he was a scrawny little guy. In fact, it might have been a boy."

"That so?" said Lester.

"At the time he just figured the guy had gone out fishing and got caught in the rain without a motor. But the next day he remembered it had been raining since noon, and nobody in his right mind would have sat on the lake from noon to dusk in that kind of downpour. Pour me a little more of that red poison, Lester. Thanks. So anyhow, the next time we have a stormy night I'm going to leave a motor on one of my boats and sit in my fish-cleaning shed by the water and wait. Make sense, Lester?"

"It might work."

Aunt Gert said, "Now wait a minute, Chad, that's foolhardy. What do you expect to do once you've caught the thief? He might have helpers along. They might push you in the lake and drown you."

"Not by a damnsight, Gert. Not if you do your part. See, as soon as they start taking the motor off the boat, I'll step out of my fish-cleaning shed with my flashlight and my deer rifle. You'll be looking out the front window, Gert, and as soon as you see the flashlight go on, you'll call the sheriff. I'll keep the rifle on them till the sheriff comes."

"Thieves are nothing to fool with," said Aunt Gert. "You leave all that business to the sheriff."

"Oh, calm down. They're as good as locked up. Now finish your wine. We have to get home."

Carrying his wine bottle, Lester followed us outside in his bare feet. "It feels like there's some weather brewing," he said.

Uncle Chad started the pickup and turned on the headlights. The tall grass and bushes around Lester's cabin were moving in the wind. A dozen large raindrops splattered on the windshield as we drove away.

In my aunt and uncle's house I fought off sleep as they gave me instructions about the use of the space heater, the kitchen stove, the telephone, the outboard motors and the boats.

I got into bed as a rumble of thunder began, and I was asleep before it ended.

Chapter 12

An alarm clock woke me at five thirty. Outside my window a woodpecker was working on a tree with a quick, hollow rap. Uncle Chad's pickup was gone. It had stopped raining and dawn was bright in the east.

I dressed, went to the kitchen, and ate four slices of homemade bread spread thick with chokecherry jelly. Then I looked through the closet and found a heavy, red-checkered jacket and a canvas hunting cap. I went outside as the sun was coming up. The grass was wet and the woods between Uncle Chad's place and Lester's dripped and sparkled in the light of the low sun. It was cold, and mist rose from the woods. I went back to the closet and found a pair of rubber boots and gloves.

I went down to the shore and unlocked the storage shed where Uncle Chad kept his outboard motors and fishing gear. The six-horse Mercurys stood in a row against one wall. On another wall were shelves and drawers full of fishing lures, reels, cans of oil, dried-up angleworms, minnow buckets, and life jackets. After slipping on a life jacket and filling a small tackle box with various hooks, sinkers, and lures, I picked out the newest looking rod and reel and stepped outside.

Near the storage shed was the fish-cleaning shed. It was a small screened-in building with a table with a hole cut in the middle. Under the hole stood a garbage can, and I knew the strong fishy smell was a good sign, for it meant that fish had recently been caught and cleaned. With Lester's guidance and a little luck, I might be cleaning my own fish there before the day was over.

I walked out on the dock. The sun was higher now. As it warmed the air, huge clouds of white mist rose from the lake. Twice near the dock I heard a splash where a fish jumped, and I saw the sparkling ripples, but I wasn't quick enough to see the fish.

Suddenly, I heard a loud flapping noise behind me, and I turned to see a giant bird heading straight for the dock. The bird and I saw each other at the same time. I ducked and the bird veered out over the water, flapping its huge wings and rising into the mist. Flying with a humped back and a crooked neck, it looked prehistoric. I left my fishing gear on the dock and crouched under a tree in case it turned and made another pass at me.

That was when Lester Flett stepped out of the woods, laughing.

"City boy survives attack by G.B.H.," he said.

"What's a G.B.H.?"

"Great blue heron. He gave you quite a start, didn't he?"

"Scared the daylights out of me."

"That heron watches the sunrise from Chad's dock every morning. Usually this time of day he has the shoreline to himself, so he didn't bother circling around and looking it over. He just came over the trees for a landing and there you stood. From now on he'll be more careful."

Lester still wore his canvas hunting coat, but he wasn't barefoot this morning. He wore an old pair of tennis shoes and a floppy straw hat with a wide brim. He carried a rod and reel, a tackle box, and a landing net, which he put into one of Uncle Chad's boats.

I asked him if herons were dangerous.

"About as dangerous as a robin. That's dangerous enough if you're a worm."

"I'm no worm."

Lester laughed. "I didn't say you were."

"It's just that wild animals make me a little jumpy."

"Animals are nothing to fear."

"What about bear? I've heard there are bear in these woods, and they attack people."

"Nonsense. What would a bear want with a person? People are too hard to chew compared to fish and berries. I've met bear in the woods when we happened to be walking the same path, and they never batted an eye. Bear are about as dangerous as blue herons, unless you meet a mother with cubs—and then you just walk the other way."

Lester stepped into Uncle Chad's storage shed and handed me a minnow bucket.

"We'll have to use one of Chad's motors," he said. "My motor is laid up. Carburetor trouble." He came out of the shed with one of my uncle's Mercurys and clamped it on the boat. Next he brought out a gas tank and connected it to the motor. Then he took the minnow bucket and waded into the water, shoes and all, to the livebox half submerged under Uncle Chad's dock.

"It isn't the animals in this world that are dangerous," said Lester as he fished for minnows in the livebox with a small net. "Bear and birds mind their own business. It's people you have to watch out for. That's why I live in the woods. Years ago I said my farewell to cities and towns, and I don't hanker to go back."

He splashed over to the boat, put in the minnow bucket, then floated the boat over to the dock and we both got in.

"At your age you wouldn't understand, but the day will come when you'll want to get away from people. You'll prefer listening to the birds to listening to small talk. You'll prefer looking at the sunrise to looking at the morning paper. That's when you'd better find yourself a place like mine."

"I know a man in St. Paul who would like to find a place like yours," I said.

"Good for him," said Lester. "He's probably the only smart man in the city."

He pulled the starter rope and we skimmed over the

water, leaving a churning wake behind us. Lester was in the stern, and I sat facing him with my back to the spray that splashed over the bow. We passed two boats from which fishermen waved to us. I waved back, Lester didn't. He kept his eyes straight ahead, squinting into the sun from under his straw hat.

We skimmed across the lake at full speed until we were a long way from shore. Then we made a wide, slow circle as Lester leaned over the side and peered into the water.

"If you see rocks, holler," he said.

The bottom gradually came into view, the green weeds and sand at first dim, then more distinct.

"Rocks," I said, and Lester cut the motor.

"Throw over the anchor," he said.

I did so, the rope playing out and holding us over what looked like the peak of an underwater rock pile. The peak appeared to be only inches below the surface, but that was only an illusion. The boat floated over the rocks without touching.

"This is where we belong," said Lester. "Put a minnow on your hook and throw it any direction."

We baited our hooks and dropped them over the side, and we left them in the water for several minutes, giving them an occasional tug. The sun was turning warm in spite of the breeze, and the boat lazily dipped and rose in the small waves.

In a few minutes Lester said, "We're off target. Pull up the anchor."

With a spurt of the motor we moved a short distance and fished again, but we didn't catch a thing.

We moved once more and put on fresh minnows. My bait had no more than settled to the bottom when I felt a light tug on the line. Then nothing. Then two quick tugs, both strong. Then nothing. Then a steady pull. I overcame my urge to reel in line. Lester told me to feed out more. It spun out steadily and then stopped.

"I've lost him," I said.

"You don't know that yet. Reel in just a little. Then if he runs with it, set the hook."

I gave the reel one turn, and the fish pulled harder than before. I stopped the line with my thumb on the reel and pulled back the rod so hard that I slipped off the seat and landed on the floor of the boat at Lester's feet. From that position I began reeling in line, inch by inch.

"No use forcing him like that," said Lester. "You'll break your line."

"But he'll get off."

"Not if you keep your line taut. Give him line if he wants it. Just don't let it go slack."

I let the reel unwind slowly under my thumb.

"What do I do now?" I asked.

"First thing you ought to do is get up off the floor."

Lester took the rod while I got back on the seat. As he handed it back to me, he said, "It's a good-sized fish. If he's a walleye, he'll tire pretty quick and you'll be able to turn him around and bring him in."

"If he isn't a walleye, what is he?"

"A northern. Or maybe a muskie. There's rumors about muskies in this lake."

The fish weakened and I was finally able to reel the

line in steadily. I got the fish close to the boat and Lester saw it first. "A walleye, all right, eight pounds at least."

The fish made a run under the boat, and I saw it roll over as I pulled up on the rod. He gave up the fight, exhausted. He was green and yellow and his belly was a dazzling white in the clear water. I could see his shadow move across the green stones. He came up and lay level by the side of the boat, his dorsal fin just breaking the water.

Lester swept the walleye up in the landing net and dumped him squirming at my feet. Then he plunged the net into the water on the opposite side and scooped out a fish of his own, another walleye, but only half the size of mine. He had the hook out of his walleye's mouth in a few seconds, then he watched me trying to get a grip on my fish. Whenever I grabbed it around the middle, it wiggled loose and thumped to the floor of the boat.

"Put your thumb and forefinger in his eyes," said Lester, showing me how he held his. It was the same way Mr. Kerr had carried his big northern. I held the walleye by the eyes and probed deep in its mouth with Lester's pliers, trying to free my hook.

"Do you think it will go ten pounds?" I asked.

"Eight or nine, not ten. Mine's four, so we're off to a good start."

My hook came loose. We baited up and continued fishing. In twenty minutes we caught four more fish, none as large as the first two, but they were all over two pounds. Lester said that was half our limit, and I suddenly realized I had forgotten to buy a fishing license.

I told Lester.

"You mean this is the first time you've gone fishing without a license?"

"First time."

Lester shook his head. "Don't worry about it," he said. He caught another walleye and held it by the eyes and twisted the hook out of its mouth.

"But a game warden might come around," I said.

"Small chance."

"But if he did he'd give me a fine and take the fish." I looked over the side of the boat at the cluster of walleyes hanging in the water on a stringer. "I never caught that many walleyes before."

"There's no danger, I tell you. In the ten years I've fished Leaf Lake, I've never bought a license." Lester turned and threw his line out behind the boat.

"Doesn't it bother you to break the law?" I asked.

"Not in the least. Fishing laws and hunting laws are no-account laws. Laws about animals aren't like laws about people."

"Not as important?"

"That's right. It's common sense that fishing without a license isn't like robbery and murder. Breaking game laws isn't serious."

Was he right? Since we'd caught the walleyes, his words seemed to take on more authority. Before we left Uncle Chad's dock, when he was telling me about preferring birds to people, I thought he was just a windy old man. But a man who can find a walleye hole in a big lake must know what he's talking about. I decided I could learn a few things from Lester.

"Lester," I said, "what would you think of a guy who squealed on his best friend?"

Lester thought for a while and then said it depended what the friend was guilty of.

"Let's say the friend is a thief," I said.

"I'd say it's a matter of conscience. Some people's consciences are like this net." He held up the landing net. "A conscience can be tight and strong and not let anything but the very smallest creatures through the holes. Or a conscience can be like a torn net—big holes that let big creatures get through."

"What's your conscience like?"

"I'd say mine is about average, torn a little here and there, somewhat ragged around the edges, but it's still tight enough to keep me honest."

"Would it tell you to squeal on your best friend?"

"If my best friend was a thief?"

"Yes."

"I don't think so. Not unless I was the one he stole from."

A cloud moved across the sky and hid the sun and made the breeze cold.

"Lester," I said, "I was once told that if you do small things wrong, like fishing without a license, then after a while you're likely to do big things wrong."

"You were told that, huh?"

"Yes. Do you believe it?"

"No. That's not true. A fellow sets up his own limit of what he'll do and what he won't do. He can go all his life and never break a big rule if he's made up his mind not to." Lester cleared his throat and spat in the lake. "That's the way it's been with me, anyhow. I might break the small rules, but I never break the big ones."

The wind freshened and the boat began to rock.

"Pull in the anchor," said Lester. "We're going home before we get wet. I see rain moving in from the east."

By the time I'd pulled up the anchor, the waves had turned into whitecaps and the boat was tipping from side to side. Lester heaved the heavy stringer into the boat, and the fish slid and twisted at his feet. He started the motor.

The boat bucked like a horse over the waves. We rode facing each other again, Lester squinting into the wind and navigating, I hunching down with my back to the water that was splashing over the bow. By the time we reached Uncle Chad's dock it was raining and we were soaked.

"Take the fish in there," said Lester, pointing to the cleaning shed. "We'll clean them first thing."

We had nearly twenty-five pounds of fish. I lugged them to the table with the hole in the middle, and Lester waded to the livebox and returned the unused minnows.

Lester made short work of the fish. From the leather sheath that hung from his belt, he drew his knife and cut, stabbed, and sliced. The flesh fell from the bones in long clean slabs. He told me to carry the filets down to the lake in the rinsed-out minnow bucket and wash them off. He kept only two small fish for himself.

"For lunch now," he said, "fry a couple slices of fish in butter, and put the rest in Chad's freezer. Don't forget to take some of it back to the city with you. City folks don't often get food as good as that."

We stepped out of the shed and into the rain. Lester picked up his fishing gear and ran toward his cabin.

"Hey, Lester," I called.

He turned.

"Thanks," I said.

He saluted, touching his hat with the long handle of his landing net, then disappeared into the woods.

I emptied the fish filets from the minnow bucket onto the dock and washed them in the waves. I put the pieces back into the bucket and stood for a moment with the rain beating down on me.

It had been the best fishing trip of my life. Setting the hook as the eight-pounder tugged. Adding fish after fish to the stringer. Riding the whitecaps. Talking man-to-man with Lester. And now standing here wet and hungry but just a few steps from dry clothes and a good meal—all these satisfying feelings swept over me like the rain.

It was nearly noon by Uncle Chad's kitchen clock. Six hours had passed like one. I took a hot bath and put on dry clothes. I fried more fish than I thought I could eat, and I ate it all.

Chapter 13

I spent the rainy afternoon reading Uncle Chad's fishing magazines and sleeping. As darkness fell, the wind increased, bringing sudden flashes of lightning and thunder.

This is the kind of weather the motor thief likes, I thought. At this very moment he was probably stealing someone's motor. I looked out the window into the dark and suddenly remembered that neither Lester nor I had put away Uncle Chad's motor when we came in from fishing. We had left it on the boat. With a simple twist of the clamp, the thief could be lifting the motor off the boat while I was standing at the window.

I put on Uncle Chad's hunting cap, jacket, and boots, which had been drying by the stove all afternoon. I checked my pocket to make sure I had the key to the storage shed. Then I hunted for a flashlight. I looked in the closet, the kitchen, the laundry room, and the bedrooms, but I didn't find one.

I turned off the kitchen light and stepped outside. The force of the wind surprised me. It was stronger than before, and it nearly pushed me off balance. The rain was lighter though, despite the rumbling of thunder.

Before I reached the shore, I heard the thud of wood on wood, and I assumed the boat Lester and I had used was banging against the dock.

Then lightning flashed and I saw in an instant two boats by the dock and a man in one of them.

After the lightning it was pitch-dark, but what I had seen was burned in my mind. A small man in a rubber parka was sitting in a boat drawn up beside Uncle Chad's boat. The two boats were rising and falling unevenly in the waves, knocking against each other, and the man had one hand on my uncle's boat.

My scalp tingled. The man had not seen me in the lightning because his back was turned, and he had not heard me approach because of the rushing wind. I crouched under the tree near the dock where Lester had found me at sunrise, and I tried to remember what Uncle Chad had planned to do in this situation. He said he would be watching with his rifle and his flashlight. I didn't have either one. And even if I had, there was no one in the house to signal to.

Lightning flashed again. The man was standing in the shallow water between the two boats. He was lifting the motor off Uncle Chad's boat. As before, all

I saw of him was the back of his rubber parka shining in the sudden light. He was small.

I knelt under the tree with my head pressed against the trunk to steady my shaking.

Another flash. The thief had already transferred the motor. It was lying in his own boat. He was pushing himself away from the dock with one foot still in the water. Then everything was black again.

I waited for another flash, but the lightning had moved on. I had seen only blackness, except for those three sudden images of the thief. It was like three stop-action photographs of a football play where you see only the beginning, the middle, and the end. I had seen that figure like a statue in three poses: reaching for the boat, transferring the motor, and shoving off.

I stayed where I was for an eternity—perhaps a minute—after the thief was swallowed up in the night. Then I ran to the house, switched on the kitchen light, and picked up the phone. There was no dial tone. I put it back on the receiver and picked it up again—still no dial tone. I tried it a half-dozen more times with no luck, then I dialed the operator anyhow. I must have dialed zero a dozen times. I was standing in a puddle of water dripping from my clothes, staring at the dead phone. The wires must be down, I thought. The storm has probably blown down a pole somewhere, and I'm cut off from the outside.

But at least I wasn't cut off from Lester Flett. With the lake so rough, the thief surely couldn't row very fast, and he would have to stay close to shore. If Lester and I were to run along the shore we might catch him. I turned off the lights and went outside.

Although Lester's cabin wasn't far, I couldn't find it. I started through the woods, but I could have done as well blindfolded. I kept tripping over vines and running into trees. Finally, I turned around and slowly found my way back to Uncle Chad's yard.

Well, now I could try either the road or the shore. The road was the sure way of getting there, but it would mean walking a quarter mile uphill to the fork and then another quarter mile down Lester's driveway. I decided to take the shore. I went down to the beach and walked along with the waves breaking over my boots, and before I knew it I stumbled over Lester's dock.

A yellow light shone through the window of Lester's cabin. I ran around to the cabin door and opened it. Nobody home. The kerosene lamp burned on the table. The yellow daisy in the wine bottle nodded in the wind. I closed the door and looked around.

A dim light shone from the old shed by the driveway. As I approached it, I could see through its open door. A shadow moved across the far wall. Lester was in there, all right.

I was ten yards from the shed and was about to yell Lester's name above the wind, when I saw something that stopped me. At my feet, lying in the dim light that fell across the ground from the doorway, was a six-horse Mercury. Uncle Chad's motor. Then a figure appeared in the center of the shed, wearing a rubber parka. It was Lester. He picked up a tarpaulin, uncovering at least a dozen outboard motors lying on the floor.

The thief was Lester.

Keeping my distance from the shed, I walked around it to the far side where the window was. I walked up to the window and looked in. Lester was standing over his loot. The motors lay at his feet, some large, some small, most of them new and shiny. Lester stepped out the door where I had been standing and he came back into the shed with Uncle Chad's motor. I backed up two or three steps so he wouldn't notice my face against the window pane.

Then I realized that the wall I was facing was flooded with light. The light was coming from behind me. I spun around and saw two headlights bouncing down Lester's driveway. I was in full view of whoever was driving. For some reason, I imagined that it was Uncle Chad and Aunt Gert looking for me, having returned home sooner than they planned. I waved my arms and shouted their names.

The driver reached the point where the driveway curves away from the shed, but he didn't turn. He drove straight for the shed. The headlights bore down on me. I leaped aside and rolled into the brush as the headlights smashed into the wall of the shed. The wall splintered and caved in. It was a van. The driver, a fat man, got out, shouting Lester's name. I went deeper into the woods, groping my way toward Uncle Chad's house.

Chapter 14

I was a long time getting back. I put my hands in front of my face and bushwhacked through the brush and branches, but I stumbled several times over tangled grass. Finally I lay on my back, panting.

Looking up, I saw a break in the clouds. Glistening moonlight surrounded me for a moment, then faded, then reappeared. Windblown clouds were hurrying under the moon and the spaces between them grew. The rain was over, but the wind was stronger and colder.

I shook, but not entirely from the cold. I was now beginning to understand how narrow my escape had been. I had nearly been smashed against the wall of the shed by that van.

I stood up and found the woods easier to travel in

the moonlight, for now I could see where I was going. I reached the edge of the woods and saw a light from my uncle's house. I was about to run toward it when I remembered I had turned off the lights when I left the house. This light was moving. Two figures—one large and one small—were entering Uncle Chad's kitchen door. They had evidently come from Lester's by way of the beach. The house lights went on, one by one, in every room. I backed off several feet into the woods and crouched behind a bush. Then the lights went off, one by one, and the two men stepped outside. They walked toward me, then stopped at the edge of the woods. I could see them in the moonlight. One was Lester. The other was one of the fattest men I'd ever seen. He must have weighed three hundred pounds.

"He must have run off in a different direction." It was Lester's voice. "He's only a kid and he's a stranger around here, so it's hard to say where he's gone to." He had more to say, but I couldn't hear it above the wind.

Then the fat man spoke. "He's got to be found, Flett. You find him while I see if the truck still runs. Bring him back to the shed and I'll haul him with me to Duluth. The boss will know what to do with him. Hurry up, now. We've got all those motors to load up yet."

The fat man took a step into the woods and stood so near me I could have touched his leg.

"Wait a minute," said Lester, stepping up to him. "That's kidnapping. I'm not going to be party to a kidnapping."

91

"What's your solution? Drown him in the lake? He's seen both of us now, and he knows what we're up to."

"I say forget him. He's a kid in the woods with no ride to town. His telephone line is cut. We'll load the motors and take off. Even if he gets brave and goes to town, he'll never go before daylight. He's scared of bear. By that time we'll be far away and rid of the motors. We're only two hundred miles from the border."

"We?"

"We. Both of us. I'll have to go with you now; the kid knows I'm the thief."

"You're going to pull up stakes?"

"I don't care where I live as long as it's in the woods. I'll find me a cabin somewhere in Canada."

"O.K., Flett. But if he ever squeals on you, you'll be sorry you didn't take care of him when you had the chance."

"If he squeals on me I'll never be found. We've got six thousand dollars' worth of motors in that shed. That's three thousand dollars apiece. The way I live, that's enough to last me for years."

The fat man started through the brush toward Lester's place. He stepped on my hand.

"Not that way," said Lester. "It's faster to follow the shore, the way we came."

When they were gone, I went into the house and stood in the dark and listened to the wind howl. I knew I was afraid, but it wasn't until I went to the sink for a glass of water that I saw I was shaking. In fact, I was gritting my teeth to keep them from chattering.

As long as I stayed out of sight I was safe. In an hour or two—however long it took to get the collapsed wall off the truck and to load six thousand dollars' worth of motors—both men would be gone. Until then I would stay in the house. Trembling.

Then I thought, they might change their minds. They might return to the house and look for me again. I ran outside and stood under the moving branches of a tall pine.

I thought about Lester, my fishing guide, my companion. What a fraud he was. All that hot air about breaking the small rules and keeping to the big ones. But he seemed to have saved my life by convincing the fat man not to look for me. What would Uncle Chad say when he found out Lester was a thief?

But how would Uncle Chad ever find out, except from me? And I had no intention of talking. I was safe now as long as I stayed out of the way. That's what I would do. Stay in the dark. Hide in a tree if necessary.

And if I hid all night, of course, I would have to keep it a secret for the rest of my life. If I spoke about it, people would want to know what I had done to stop the thieves.

I climbed the pine tree. I would hide and never speak about it as long as I lived. Halfway up I sat on a branch with one arm around the trunk, which was sticky with pitch. It wasn't long before I was aching all over. I knew I couldn't sit on the branch all night.

I jumped to the ground and ran up the driveway toward the highway. I was on my way to Pinecone to find the sheriff. Whether it was my conscience or my aching muscles that drove me out of the pine tree, I don't know. But once I started for town, I had no doubt that I was doing the right thing. When I reached the highway I stopped to catch my breath, standing with my hands on my knees. I waited for a car to come along.

Two cars passed, but in the wrong direction. Finally a car approached in the direction I was going, but putting my thumb out didn't even slow it down.

I decided to start walking and running toward Pinecone, hoping to find a house with a phone along the way. I covered nearly a mile before more cars approached from behind me. I put my thumb out to three pairs of headlights, but they didn't stop. Then a single light approached, and what I assumed at first to be a motorcycle turned out to be a van with the front end smashed in and one headlight dead. It stopped for me. The door opened. Lester jumped out. The fat man got out on the driver's side.

Lester and I faced each other for a full second as the fat man came around the front of the van. I think Lester was giving me a chance to run, but I was paralyzed for that second and the fat man grabbed for my arm.

I shook loose and ran down into the ditch and up a slope into the woods. I tripped on a fallen tree and landed flat on my stomach. I dared not get up because the men were too close. I squirmed around to look behind me. Lester was entering the woods, followed by the fat man. Behind them the van stood on the highway with the headlight on and the motor running.

Lester stopped a few feet away from me and waited for the fat man to catch up. Then he said, "This way," and led him deeper into the woods. Lester may have seen me. I'll never know for sure.

I sat up. I wanted to run for the truck and drive it to town, but I couldn't see how far into the woods the men had gone. What if they came back and caught me as I was trying to shift gears? Shifting gears always gave me trouble. Listening for the men didn't work because I couldn't hear them over the wind that was moaning and whistling all around.

I decided to run for the truck. I ran down the slope and up out of the ditch and around to the driver's side. I listened for a moment and heard nothing but the wind and the clattering engine. No shouts.

I got in. The right-hand door was closed, and I reached over and pressed down the lock. The driver's door I left ajar, afraid to slam it because of the noise it would make. I felt around with my feet. Just as I expected, there were three pedals—gas, brake, and clutch. That meant no automatic shift. I felt around the steering wheel for the gearshift lever, but it wasn't there. It was sticking up from the floor beside my leg. I had no idea how to shift it. But now any gear was better than neutral. I pulled the stick toward me as I pushed in the clutch. The stick moved easily and I slowly let out the clutch to see what gear I was in. The van began to jerk, and by the light from the dim headlight I saw that I was slowly jerking along in reverse.

I pushed in the clutch again and brought the stick

out of reverse with a rasping and scratching of gears. That would surely bring the men running. I shifted to another slot, let out the clutch, and pressed hard on the gas. This had to be a forward gear. The van moved forward, but only in jerks. I leaned forward over the steering wheel to help it along. I pumped the clutch and pressed the gas to the floorboard. The clatter of the engine rose to a scream and then died. I must have been in third gear—not enough power to pull a truckload of motors from a dead stop.

There was a face at the right-hand window. It was the fat man's face. I slammed my door and locked it. I felt around for the ignition key. Suddenly a noise like thunder filled the cab. The fat man had smashed a rock against the right-hand window. The window remained in place, but it had a thousand shatter-streaks in it.

I found the ignition and started the engine. As I shifted the stick to another slot, the rock struck the window again and broke it open. The rock fell into the seat beside me. By this time the van was moving, and the fat man was running alongside. He put his arm through the broken window and reached for the lock. I picked up speed and the jagged glass cut his arm. I thought I was away from him, but at the last moment he jumped up on the front bumper and heaved himself up past the windshield and onto the roof of the van.

The highway curved left and right through the woods, and I drove as fast as the curves would allow. I saw the man reach down from the roof and feel for the lock in the broken window. He found the lock and pulled it up. Then the arm disappeared. He could do no more at the moment. It would take an acrobat to open the door and swing himself inside at the speed I was going. He couldn't reach me until I stopped.

After I had driven about five minutes, the country opened up with more fields than woods, and the highway straightened out. Ahead I saw the lights of Pinecone. I pressed harder on the accelerator.

As soon as I slowed down at the city limits the fat man put one foot on the sill of the broken window. Whether he was about to jump off or try to climb inside, I didn't know. I speeded up again and pressed on the horn. He climbed back on the roof.

I followed the highway to its intersection with Main Street. I screeched around the corner and raced down the street, honking and shouting, "Sheriff! Police!" Along Main Street there were streetlights, but no activity. I thought it must have been midnight or later.

Under a streetlight in the second block, an old man hobbled to the curb to see what the noise was about. I slowed down, honked, and shouted, "Police," at him through the broken window. The fat man's foot appeared on the window sill again, but it withdrew as I stepped on the gas. Two blocks further on I ran out of Main Street. I slowed down to make a U-turn, and I lost the fat man. He leaped from the roof and landed sprawling in the street. I drove back the way I had come, honking steadily, but only the old man, peering at me from under the same streetlight, took notice.

On my right I saw the lighted marquee of the Pinecone Theater. I pulled into the no-parking space and turned off the ignition. I got out and stood on the sidewalk, looking down the street, but there was no sign of the fat man.

In the lobby a lady sat in a glass cage eating popcorn. The clock over her head said eight thirty. I asked her to call the sheriff.

Chapter 15

The sheriff's office was in the old brick jail next to the old brick courthouse. The sheriff and his wife lived in an apartment at the back of the jail. He was a bald man with thick glasses, and she was a gum-chewing woman with dangling gold earrings. Both the sheriff and his wife grew excited as I told my story. He kept running his hand over his bald head, and she chewed her gum so hard her earrings danced.

The sheriff called in two deputies by phone and two-way radio, and he alerted the highway patrol and the local police force, which consisted of two men and a German shepherd. He told them to go through the streets and alleys of Pinecone in search of the fat man.

The sheriff's wife sat down at a rickety typewriter

and I told my story once more as she typed. It turned out to be seven pages long. I signed my name to it.

The sheriff said I should stay in the office for an hour or two, so if Lester and the fat man were brought in I could identify them. I said I would be glad to stay all night if necessary. I wasn't eager to spend the night alone at Uncle Chad's.

His wife sensed my feelings. "I think this boy should be a guest of the county after what he's done. The jail is empty and the V.I.P. cell has clean linen."

"How would you like to spend the night in jail?" the sheriff asked me.

"There's nothing I'd like better," I said, "but I should be watching my Uncle Chad's place."

"Don't worry about Chad's place. I'm having that area patrolled around the clock in case Lester is still out there."

Two deputies showed up, and the sheriff told them to drive the van to the courthouse and unload the outboard motors and store them in the basement. "Write down the serial number from each motor, along with the make and horsepower, then check your list with our files of stolen motors, and then call up the owners. But tell them not to expect their motors back for a few days. We'll need them as evidence."

I was given a cup of cocoa, then I was shown through a door that led to a row of cells. The largest cell was mine. A pair of pajamas, still hot from the iron, lay on the bed.

I undressed and turned off the light in the cell and

got into the squeaky bed. A dim light from the corridor cast striped shadows on the wall over my head. I fell asleep and dreamed that I was standing on the dock at sunrise. A great blue heron came over the trees and I had to leap off the dock to get out of his way. Before I hit the water I woke up with a jerk. I heard voices coming over the two-way radio in the sheriff's office. I heard the howl of the wind outside my barred window. I went back to sleep and did not dream.

At seven in the morning I woke up and looked out the window of my cell. The storm was over and the sun was shining. I had breakfast with the sheriff and his wife—bacon, eggs, fried potatoes, and cake—and when we finished eating, the sheriff said, "Come with me, I want to show you something."

He led me up a flight of iron steps to another row of cells. I don't know what I expected to see, but when we came to the cell with the fat man in it, I was so startled I jumped.

The sheriff saw my reaction and said, "That's all I wanted to know. We got the right man."

He turned to leave, but I lingered for a moment, looking into the cell. The fat man sat on his bunk, glaring up at me. His face was bruised, perhaps from leaping off the van, perhaps from struggling with the police. It was the same frightening face I had glimpsed through the window of the truck when I was trying to pick up speed and he was running alongside. But now he had a bandage over one eye and he didn't look so dangerous.

He gave me a bitter sneer. I turned and followed the sheriff downstairs.

"What's his name?" I asked.

"His name is Bruno Rock. He's been in prison twice for armed robbery. We found him about midnight, hiding in a garage."

"What about Lester?"

"No sign of Lester. He'll be harder to find. He's a brush rabbit."

"At least you got the more dangerous of the two. I don't think Lester would have tried to kill me. This guy tried to smash me against the shed with his truck. And I'm sure he would have smashed my skull with a rock if I hadn't picked up speed just in time."

"Bruno Rock denies everything. He says he never saw that truck before. He says he never met a man named Lester Flett. He says he was hitchhiking through town last night and got tired and bedded down in a garage."

"He's lying."

"Of course he's lying. But he's forcing us to bring him to trial, and you will have to testify."

"My word against his?"

"Yes, you're the only eyewitness. Just tell your story in court the way you told it in my office last night. It's nothing to worry about."

"When is the trial?"

"Not for a month or so. Court convenes in October, so that means you'll be up here during the hunting season. Perfect timing. Your Uncle Chad will probably take you out on a duck shoot. Pinecone County will pay your way up from St. Paul."

"I'll come."

"Your Uncle Chad is the best shot I know of. He's got an old single-shot Winchester that never misses."

"Speaking of Uncle Chad, he and Aunt Gert are due back today. I suppose I should be out at the resort when they get back."

"Fine. I'll give you a ride."

He dropped me off at the resort and said I would be notified of the trial in early October. He shook my hand and said I had done a great service to everybody on Leaf Lake and he admired my courage.

"I guess I didn't tell you that I was tempted to hide in a tree," I said.

"Don't feel bad," he said. "I've been in this business a long time and I still get the feeling now and then that I'd like to hide in a tree. You don't learn about courage without learning about fear."

After he left I walked through the woods to Lester's cabin. A deputy I hadn't seen before was sitting in a patrol car under a pine tree. He said if I was looking for Lester he wasn't home.

"I know it," I said. "I was the last one to see him."

"Are you the kid that drove the truck to town?"

"That's me."

"I bet that was the longest four miles you ever drove."

"It was. And the first ten feet were the worst. I had trouble shifting gears. Do you mind if I look around?"

"Go ahead."

Lester's door must have been open all night. Besides the usual mess Lester lived in, the floor was covered with dead leaves, blown in by the wind. The wild flower on the table had withered, its blossom hanging dead over the mouth of the wine bottle. Lester's shotgun was still hanging on the wall, but the rifle was gone. He must have returned for it, before he ran away. As far as I could tell, it was the only thing he took with him. He was traveling light.

"I suppose the sooner Lester is caught, the sooner you can go home," I said to the deputy.

"Lester will never be caught. We'll look through the bushes for two, three days as a formality, but Lester is like a coyote. He knows the woods better than we do. It's only twenty miles to the border, you know. I bet right now he's sitting on the shore of some Canadian lake, planning to build himself a cabin like this one here. He's got three, four weeks to do it before it turns real cold."

By the time Uncle Chad and Aunt Gert got home, their yard was full of cars—lake people who'd heard the news and had come over to thank me and ask questions. I told the story dozens of times and when the last car pulled out of the yard, I sat down with my aunt and uncle for a midnight snack.

Aunt Gert was worried about Lester.

"That old sneak thief?" said Uncle Chad. "I never did have any respect for him. He could make a good batch of chokecherry wine, but that was about his only contribution to mankind."

"Don't talk like that, Chad," said Aunt Gert. "There

was hardly a day went by that he didn't pay us a visit. He was like family."

"Well, he's not like family any more, thanks to Tommy here."

"Tom," I said.

"Don't you have any pity for the man?" asked Aunt Gert.

"Out of sight, out of mind," said Uncle Chad. "He's a sneak thief and a fugitive from justice, and he ought to be strung up. But he's left behind a perfectly good cabin for anybody who wants to live in it. Tommy, how would you like to move into that cabin? Isn't that your idea of paradise?"

"No, not exactly. I've got unfinished business in St. Paul. Like two years of high school. But I know somebody who's looking for a place like Lester's. My old boss, Mr. Kerr. He wants to spend his retirement up here in the woods."

"Tell him to move right up," said Uncle Chad. "If you say he's an all right guy he can have the place rent free. What do you say, Gert?"

"Yes, indeed. I don't like to see that cabin stand empty. It makes me sad for Lester. The sooner somebody moves in, the better."

"Mr. Kerr might need some help with firewood and things like that," I said. "His left arm isn't much use to him ever since he got beat up."

"Has he got money to live on?" asked Uncle Chad.

"He's pretty well off."

"Then he should insulate the cabin and put in a gas stove to heat the place. I'll help him do it. He'll be warm as toast all winter, and we won't have to chop any wood."

"Good idea," I said. "Can I tell him the news when I get back to the city tomorrow?"

"Tell him the cabin is his, Tommy."

"Tom," I said.

Chapter 16

So here I sit in the Marshall Avenue branch of the St. Paul Public Library. I'm on my third ballpoint pen. The first one ran out of ink on page forty-seven, and the second one dried up on page eighty. If I had known it was going to take me sixteen chapters to tell this story, I doubt if I'd've had the courage to start. I've been here nine days. School starts tomorrow.

Nine days ago, about noon, I arrived home from Pinecone, with my frozen walleye melting through the newspaper I'd wrapped it in. I told my folks about my adventure, and just as I'd expected, Dad, in his undershirt, led me up and down the hallways of the apartment building and had me tell the story to all the neighbors. Mother followed along. Every time I got to the part about Bruno Rock trying to crush me with his truck, Dad would say, "See, Margaret? What did I tell you? Human nature is the same in the country as it is in the city." The neighbors shook my hand and they shook Dad's hand and they consoled Mother, who looked fretful.

After that, I walked over to the police station to report Mouse. It was not only my duty as a citizen, it was my duty as Mouse's friend. I wanted to put an end to his life of crime before he ended up like Bruno Rock. I walked to the station—but I didn't go in. I paused on the front step and tried to think of what I would tell Mr. Afton when he asked me why I had waited so long— why I'd been concealing evidence all summer. I couldn't think of a good excuse, so I decided to save that whole affair till later. I went around the side of the police station and down the alley and up to Mr. Kerr's apartment, above what is now Papa Tino's Pizza Parlor.

Mr. Kerr was standing at his sink cleaning half a dozen tiny perch he'd caught in the Mississippi. The use of his left arm seemed to be coming back. When I told him about Lester Flett's cabin, he had me sit down and draw a diagram of the place, including the door, the windows, the cupboard, the cot—everything I could remember. I even drew the daisy in the wine bottle. He plans to move to the cabin in October when I go to Pinecone for the trial. We'll go up together in his Ford.

Leaving Mr. Kerr, I set off for the police station again. But the dime store was closer, so I went there instead and bought this notebook. Then I stopped at Tilbury's for a Coke.

Mouse was sitting at the counter. I was glad to see him. He was the same old Mouse.

"Man, you sure missed the boat by not going to the Labor Day races," he said. "Every good-looking girl on the face of the earth was there. I met a girl from Milwaukee you wouldn't believe. She's got cousins here in St. Paul, and the next time she comes to visit she's going to call me up. Listen, Tom, there's another big race coming up the first weekend in October, and this is your last chance. Either you come along with me or I won't ask you again. There's plenty of other guys that want to go with me, now that I've got my own car. Have you seen it yet? It's over there across the street. That red Chevy. Four years old. Runs like new. I suppose you're still driving that old bomb of Mr. Kerr's. Listen, what do you say about the October races?"

"I'm going back to Pinecone in October."

"Back to Pinecone? Man, you sure are turning into a country boy. I suppose next time I see you you'll be wearing a coonskin cap. What's going on in Pinecone in October?"

I told Mouse the whole story. He liked the part about Lester Flett's getting away. Then I showed him the notebook I had just bought and I told him I was going to put the story of my summer in the notebook before school started. I had nine days to do it. I was going to be a full-fledged junior.

"You're a sad case, Tom. Sixteen years old and still doing rinky-dink assignments for old Singleton. Don't you ever get the urge to bust out of your boyhood?"

A question like that is hard to answer. I could have told him that everybody busts out of his boyhood in his own way, at his own pace, and that he had chosen one way and I had chosen another. But I never think of good answers like that till it's too late.

I said, "Aren't you going back to school?"

"School! Listen, I can't imagine ever going back to school. My summer job has turned into a year-round job. I'm in with a bigger outfit now—you might call it a federation. We've expanded our operations out to the suburbs. I couldn't afford to go back to school and give up the money I'm making. I pay the grocery bills at home and I make monthly payments on that Chevy. And you ought to see my new stereo."

I looked him in the eye. "Tell me about your job, Mouse."

He laughed. "You wouldn't be interested. If I thought you'd be interested, I'd tell you."

"Is there any future in it, Mouse?" I wanted him to think about where his crime was leading him.

He laughed again, and stood up to leave. He said, "Is there any future in looking at your spit through a microscope?"

On his way out he paid for my Coke—with stolen money.

When Mouse had driven away, I left Tilbury's and went to the police station. It was now or never. I went inside and found Mr. Afton in the front office. I had to remind him who I was.

"Oh, yes," he said. "The grocery store break-in."

I asked him if we could talk in private, and he led me

down the hall to his office. "Now what can I do for you?" he said, settling behind his desk.

What I did next was the most difficult chore of my life. I swear it was easier driving those four miles to Pinecone with Bruno Rock clinging to the truck. I took a deep breath and said, "One of the guys who broke into the grocery store was Mouse—Morris Brown, Apartment 512, 1420 Third Street. I didn't see his face, but I recognized his voice."

Mr. Afton jumped out of his chair. "You mean you knew this ever since June 16?"

"Mouse Brown is my best friend. At least he was. It didn't seem right to squeal on my best friend."

Mr. Afton sat down again and gripped the edge of his desk. "That's no excuse at all. Do you realize that withholding evidence is a crime, that I could bring charges against you?"

"But Mouse helps support his family. His mother is temperamental, his father is kind of crazy, and his little brothers look up to him . . ."

"Those excuses aren't good enough. You've given him the whole summer to rob people and beat up people and who knows what else. Now you go straight home and stay close to your phone. If you go someplace, leave word. I'll want to talk to you as soon as we arrest this Brown."

"All right. But while I'm at it I might as well tell you something else. The other robber was a guy I remember from school—an older guy with a police record named Bob Peabody."

Mr. Afton closed his eyes. "Bob Peabody is no

stranger to the police," he said, "and this brings you up to two counts of withholding evidence."

"Will I have to testify against Mouse?" I asked.

"Of course. It's your duty as a citizen."

"And he'll probably hate me for the rest of his life."

"He might hate you. But if we get him in time to turn his life around, he'll eventually have to admit that getting caught was the best thing that could have happened to him. When he realizes that, he won't hate you any more."

"He won't go to prison, will he?"

"Why shouldn't he go to prison? He's a criminal."

"I mean he's only sixteen. Won't he be put on probation?"

"In whose custody? It doesn't sound like his parents could assume responsibility for him. If he's sixteen one of two things will happen to him, depending on how much crime he's been involved in, and how lenient the judge is. He'll be sent either to the Reformatory in St. Cloud or—if he's lucky—to the State Training School in Red Wing. If Brown cooperates with the police, I'll recommend Red Wing to the judge."

"How long will he be in for?"

"I can't say how long. A lot depends on his attitude. If he's sent to Red Wing, and if his attitude is good, he might be kept there only for the school year and released in the spring. Now you go home and let me get to work on this business."

"Mr. Afton, I've got one more question."

"Yes?"

"If I did the right thing how come I feel so rotten?"

He waved me away, saying, "Stay close to the phone."

I took my notebook home and tried writing, but it was too hot in the apartment, so I came over here to the library, where it's air-conditioned and my hand doesn't stick to the paper.

Mouse was arrested that same afternoon. I wasn't called back to the station to give evidence against him because as soon as he was arrested, he confessed. He not only confessed, he also agreed to give evidence against his accomplices, and he led the police to a ring of eight thieves and fences, including Bob Peabody.

Two days later, Mr. Afton called to tell me that the judge had heard Mouse's case.

"So soon?" I said. In Pinecone they weren't going to get around to Bruno Rock until October.

He said, "We pride ourselves on swift justice around here. Morris Brown has been sentenced to one year in the Red Wing Training School." He paused to hear my reaction, but I could think of nothing to say, so he moved on to the next item of business: He reprimanded me for withholding evidence, then he thanked me for giving it.

"Mr. Afton," I said, "I still feel rotten."

"Listen, Tom, you did right. Don't start doubting that. Sometimes doing right is harder than doing wrong—but never in the long run. If you feel rotten about reporting Mouse, think how rotten you'd feel if you didn't report him and after a year or two he was picked up for something worse, like murder. Believe me, I've been a cop long enough to know that's what would happen to him eventually. If Morris Brown ever makes anything of his life it will be because of what you've done. Now if you're still feeling bad about it, I suggest you go down to the city jail and see him before he's taken to Red Wing. Clear the air. Tell him you're concerned about him. Tell him you turned him in because you wanted to save his life."

"You think he'll see it that way?"

"I think so. He's been very cooperative with us, and he may listen to reason."

So, early the next morning, carrying a pass from Mr. Afton, I went downtown to the city jail to see Mouse. In the juvenile wing I was shown to his cell at the end of a long, gloomy corridor. Mouse was lying on his bunk, smoking and listening to a little transistor radio he had on the pillow next to his ear. He glanced at me, then looked away.

Through the bars, I said, "What happened was for the best, Mouse. I squealed on you for your own good. Some day you'll thank me for it." I don't know if he heard me or not. He didn't turn down his radio.

"I hope you understand," I said. "I did what I had to do."

At that, Mouse got up off his bunk and spit in my face. He spit right in my eye.

That evening Dad and I went to Met Stadium to watch the Twins play Texas. The loser would gain sole possession of last place in the American League West, so you might say it was a crucial game. When we got home (the Twins won 8–2), Dad told me to come up on the roof with him and tell him what was eating me. He said I had been acting gloomy lately and that I had watched the whole ballgame as though it were a funeral.

We went up on the dark roof and sat on our lawn chairs with our feet up on the parapet. The street below was quiet and dark, but we could see the lights and hear the traffic over on Marshall.

"It's about Mouse," I said, in the dark.

"What about Mouse?" My folks knew most of the story already. What I hadn't told them, Mouse's mother had told them over the phone. Now I filled Dad in on Mouse's last gesture—spitting in my face.

"How did you feel when he spit at you?"

"Mad," I said.

"How do you feel about it now?"

"Mad. And rotten."

"Are you as mad now as you were when it happened?"

I shrugged. "I guess not, but I don't feel any less rotten."

"Do you know why Mouse spit on you?"

"Sure, I squealed on him."

"Do you understand why he had to spit on you?"

"What do you mean, had to?"

"He spit on you to maintain a little bit of pride. You see, Tom, a jail cell is one of the most humiliating places in the world. If there is a more humiliating place than a jail it's a State Training School, where you're watched over day and night like a baby in a nursery. Here's a boy sixteen years old, and just about the time he feels himself growing into adulthood and achieving all the independence that goes with it, he suddenly finds himself in jail and about to be sent to the State Training School. He's humiliated. And what makes it worse, he knows it's his own fault."

"You think he'll ever want to be friends again?"

"Yes, someday, perhaps. His resentment could eventually dry up and disappear—just like your anger at being spit at. All it takes is time."

Nine days of writing. My right hand is numb and my penmanship is getting sloppier by the page. The librarian—a young woman in a purple pantsuit—has just cleared her throat, which means it's almost closing time. She starts clearing her throat every night at ten minutes to nine. She's turned out the lights in the stacks and switched off the air-conditioner. Now she's propping open the big front door. And now a fresh breeze has swept into the library—a crisp breeze that is turning up the corner of this page as I write—a cool breeze that is bringing with it the unmistakable smell of autumn.

As I said on page one, Mr. Singleton—
Summer is over.

About the Author

Jon Hassler was born in Minneapolis in 1933. He received degrees from St. John's University in Minnesota, where he was Regents' Professor Emeritus, and from the University of North Dakota. Jon Hassler was the author of twelve widely acclaimed novels: *Staggerford, Simon's Night, The Love Hunter, A Green Journey, Grand Opening, North of Hope, Dear James, Rookery Blues, The Dean's List, The Staggerford Flood, The Staggerford Murders,* and *The New Woman*. He died in 2008.